It's just revenge with him, Nora thought.

A power struggle. I'd be a trophy. A tool. A means of causing humiliation.

His next words only confirmed her supposition. "Naturally you'd have to move into my house. You'd be expected to serve as a good wife, despite the limits that would be placed on our sex life. That would mean making my tea and packing my lunch. Scrubbing my back. Sleeping with me in my bed whenever I want you there."

"I don't understand," Nora faltered.

"Let me repeat my terms. Sex once, at a time of my choosing, and a year of marriage. At the end of that time, I'd have my revenge on your family. My stock in Braet & Company would be yours. I'll be leaving town around 11:00 a.m. Let me know what you decide."

He'd given her less than twenty-four hours to choose her fate....

Dear Reader,

Traditionally June is the month for weddings, so Silhouette Romance cordially invites you to enjoy our promotion JUNE BRIDES, starting with Suzanne Carey's *Sweet Bride of Revenge*. In this sensuously powerful VIRGIN BRIDES tale, a man forces the daughter of his nemesis to marry him, never counting on falling in love with the enemy....

Up-and-comer Robin Nicholas delivers a touching BUNDLES OF JOY titled *Man, Wife and Little Wonder*. Can a denim-clad, Harley-riding bad boy turn doting dad and dedicated husband? Find out in this classic marriage-of-convenience romance! Next, Donna Clayton's delightful duo MOTHER & CHILD continues with the evocative title *Who's the Father of Jenny's Baby?* A woman awakens in the hospital to discover she has amnesia—and she's pregnant! Problem is, *two* men claim to be the baby's father—her estranged husband...and her husband's brother!

Granted: Wild West Bride is the next installment in Carol Grace's BEST-KEPT WISHES series. This richly Western romance pairs a toughened, taut-muscled cowboy and a sophisticated city gal who welcomes his kisses, but will she accept his ring? For a fresh spin on the bridal theme, try Alice Sharpe's *Wife on His Doorstep*. An about-to-be bride stops her wedding to the wrong man, only to land on the doorstep of the strong, silent ship captain who was to perform the ill-fated nuptials.... And in Leanna Wilson's latest Romance, *His Tomboy Bride*, Nick Latham was *supposed* to "give away" childhood friend and bride-to-be Billie Rae—not claim the transformed beauty as his own!

We hope you enjoy the month's wedding fun, and return each and every month for more classic, emotional, heartwarming novels from Silhouette Romance.

Enjoy!

Joan Marlow Golan

Joan Marlow Golan
Senior Editor Silhouette Romance

Please address questions and book requests to:
Silhouette Reader Service
U.S.: 3010 Walden Ave., P.O. Box 1325, Buffalo, NY 14269
Canadian: P.O. Box 609, Fort Erie, Ont. L2A 5X3

VIRGIN BRIDES

SWEET BRIDE
OF REVENGE

Suzanne
Carey

Silhouette
ROMANCE™
Published by Silhouette Books
America's Publisher of Contemporary Romance

SILHOUETTE BOOKS

ISBN 0-373-19300-9

SWEET BRIDE OF REVENGE

Printed in U.S.A.

Books by Suzanne Carey

Silhouette Romance

A Most Convenient
  Marriage #633
Run, Isabella #682
Virgin Territory #736
The Baby Contract #777
Home for Thanksgiving #825
Navajo Wedding #855
Baby Swap #880
Dad Galahad #928
Marry Me Again #1001
The Male Animal #1025
The Daddy Project #1072
Father by Marriage #1120
The Bride Price #1247
Sweet Bride of Revenge #1300

Silhouette Desire

Kiss and Tell #4
Passion's Portrait #69
Mountain Memory #92
Leave Me Never #126
Counterparts #176
Angel in His Arms #206
Confess to Apollo #268
Love Medicine #310
Any Pirate in a Storm #368

Silhouette Books

Silhouette Summer Sizzlers 1993
"Steam Bath"

Fortune's Children
Mystery Heiress

Silhouette Intimate Moments

Never Say Goodbye #330
Strangers When We Meet #392
True to the Fire #435
Eleanora's Ghost #518
Whose Baby? #715

SUZANNE CAREY

is a former reporter and magazine editor who prefers to
write romance novels because they add to the sum total
of love in the world.

Dear Reader,

The scrupulously maintained virginity of top model Nora Braet, heroine of *Sweet Bride of Revenge,* is a boon to be cherished in today's world. Yet she chooses to relinquish it in a temporary marriage of convenience to sexy multimillionaire businessman Seiji Amundsen in hopes of giving her beloved but ill aunt Maggie a reason for living.

Her courage and dawning sensuality, along with Seiji's transformation from a bitter, vengeance-minded "outsider" to the kind of resonant, loving man any woman would adore, were part of a plot that began to weave itself into my thoughts as we flew high above the Pacific Ocean to Japan in November 1995.

With my scratch pad stashed in the overhead luggage compartment, I began sketching out the conflict that would keep them apart, yet ultimately bring them together, on a perfume ad torn from a magazine. Later, as my husband and I strolled the grounds of Kyoto's Kinkakuji Temple, Nora and Seiji kept pace, whispering additional details of their story into my ears.

Now the book's finished and in your hands. I hope you'll enjoy meeting them as much as I did—and that the old-fashioned but much-prized virtue that animates it and the VIRGIN BRIDES series generally will make it all the more memorable for you. Happy reading!

Suzanne Carey

Chapter One

"Here...read this. You'll see what we're up against," Stephanie Braet said with more than her usual emphasis, thrusting a copy of *Worldview* magazine into Nora's lap as their older sister, Darien, frowned over her coffee cup.

A clone of *Time* and *Newsweek* except for its strong international slant, *Worldview* was known for its intimate portraits of world leaders and global business executives. The issue Stephanie had handed her was approximately a month out of date. It had been folded open to a story about multimillionaire industrialist and corporate raider Nels S. Amundsen—the man they'd have to deal with if they wanted to save the family department-store chain for their aunt Maggie's sake.

Aware of Amundsen's existence thanks to a distant family connection, even before he'd initiated his push to take over Braet & Company, twenty-five-year-old Nora had never met him personally. Pushing back her natural auburn hair with an absent gesture and crossing the long, shapely legs that had helped make her a star on New York fashion runways, she glanced first at the photo that accompanied the text.

His looks were international and hard to place—thick, dark brown hair worn fashionably long though it was neatly styled and trimmed, Western features except for the faint suggestion of Asian heritage around his enigmatic gray eyes. He appeared to have the height and muscular build of his Scandinavian ancestors.

A half smile tugged at the corners of his mouth, hinting at both sensuality and stubbornness. A powerful thirty-four-year-old wheeler-dealer who clearly knew what he wanted and was committed to getting it, the financial raider she and her sisters had met to discuss appeared to stare back at her from the page with an emotional intensity that gave her goose bumps.

So this is the man who's positioned himself to take over Braet & Company by buying up as much of its outstanding stock as he could lay his hands on, she thought. Ironic, isn't it, that we're *related*...half cousins once removed if I've got the connection straight.

In Nora's opinion, Amundsen's decision to rub their noses in a hostile takeover probably had arisen from a sense of injury stemming from that distant relationship. No doubt the refusal of the American descendants of his grandfather, Jerrold Braet, who was Nora's great-grandfather, as well, to have anything to do with his Japanese grandmother or his widowed, part-Japanese mother had grated on him for as long as he could remember.

Well, what does he expect? she asked herself. He must realize the scandal of Jerrold's divorce from Katherine Wells Braet to marry his pregnant Japanese girlfriend would leave a lasting mark. Besides, there's been nothing deliberate about it on the part of our generation. Almost fifty-six years have gone by. We're too detached from what happened to have snubbed anyone intentionally.

Tearing her gaze from Amundsen's photo with reluctance, Nora began to read the article, looking for a chink in his armor. She couldn't seem to find one, unless she counted his alienation from the Braets and his upbringing in ultrahomogenous Japan as a part-foreigner—a social outcast of sorts despite his late father's wealth and prominence.

"Amundsen's middle initial stands for Seiji (pronounced say-gee), a Japanese given name that Amundsen prefers to use except when he signs official documents," the writer stated. "He's also been dubbed 'The Falconer'—some say because of the strong control he exerts over his many enterprises while allowing those subordinates who merit it a measure of creative freedom and trust.

"The nickname probably also refers to his practice of keeping falcons at his Japanese country estate. His uncompromising business philosophy fits the description that hobby paints of him to perfection. Few would deny that the sport of falconry has a predatory connotation. And, as rivals who've butted heads with him will tell you, Amundsen can't easily be dissuaded from his purpose of the moment. When he's 'waiting on' for his prey to flush, as one American associate put it in falconry terms, he's tenacious, unbelievably persistent…"

A well-known *Worldview* staffer who frequently did double duty as a television talk-show panelist, the writer went on to describe his subject's international credentials.

"An inveterate traveler with financial interests around the globe, Seiji Amundsen is one quarter each Danish, Norwegian, Japanese and American of European descent," he wrote. "He's a true citizen of the world though he was brought up mostly in Kyoto by his half-American, half-Japanese mother and his late father, Peter Amundsen, a Norwegian-Danish shipping tycoon.

"The latter made Japan his home after marrying Aiko Braet, the daughter of Yukiko Kurosawa, a young Japanese woman of good family and Jerrold Braet, who—in 1923—founded the American department-store chain his grandson's conglomerate is currently attempting to acquire. The two met when Braet, then fifty-seven, was caught in Japan as World War II broke out. Braet divorced his wife of many years to marry Kurosawa, twenty-two, after she became pregnant."

I can't approve of what Jerrold did, Nora thought. To me, marriage is sacred. I have zero tolerance for infidelity no matter what the circumstances. Great-grandmother Katherine must have been terribly hurt.

Still, she saw no reason for the Braets to continue shunning Aiko and her son, Seiji, who'd had nothing to do with Jerrold's transgression. With a little shake of her head, she continued to read.

"Educated in Japan through the equivalent of eighth grade," the writer continued, "Amundsen graduated from prep schools and universities in England, Denmark and the U.S. He has an M.B.A. from Harvard Business School. It's said that though he can be warm and friendly, his heart seems to have become hardened by growing up as an *ainoko* (part-Japanese, part-foreigner). Among the Japanese, it's not a complimentary term. In a way, though he's a very wealthy, very

powerful man, Amundsen belongs everywhere and nowhere…''

Despite her firm opposition to what he was planning,
Nora couldn't help resonating with compassion at what
sounded like Seiji Amundsen's essential loneliness
even as her instinctive attraction to him deepened. I
wonder what it would be like to nestle in those strong
arms, feel that marauding mouth plundering mine? she
thought, glancing back at his photograph.

A moment later she was admonishing herself. You
can't afford to feel sympathy for him, she thought. Or
fascination of any sort. Considering what he's trying to
do, to the company and Aunt Maggie, unswerving opposition would be more appropriate.

The fact that Braet & Company was ripe for the
picking wasn't Seiji Amundsen's fault, of course. For
several years, the venerable department-store chain
owned by the Braet family had been in financial trouble. Too much debt, taken on in the eighties for the
purpose of expansion, and a subsequently sagging retail
market had caused Braet's profits to be eaten up by
interest payments.

As the company's chief executive officer, the sisters'
fifty-three-year-old aunt, Maggie Braet, was struggling
to restore it to solvency and profitability. Twice divorced and childless, she was also fighting cancer. Like
Stephanie and Darien, Nora feared that, if Maggie lost
the company, she'd cease battling to regain her health,
as well.

That can't be allowed to happen! she pledged.

Her green eyes glittering with a resolve that would
have done Seiji Amundsen proud, she raised them to
her sisters' expectant faces. ''What do you propose we
do about this?'' she asked.

Neither Stephanie nor Darien answered for a moment.

They and Nora had decided to meet in Maggie's condominium, which overlooked Lake Union, a wide spot in the waterway that cut through the heart of Seattle from Lake Washington to Puget Sound, because Darien's apartment near the hospital was cramped. Plus she had a roommate who worked nights. Driving up to Stephanie's place near Snoqualmie would have taken too much time. Besides, Maggie had given each of them a key. It had been easy to arrange.

Beneath their aunt's third-floor balcony, which could be accessed by sliding-glass doors, a flock of slender sailboat masts bobbed on choppy, slate gray water beneath lowering clouds. Though she'd grown up with a healthy dose of similar weather, the gloom only depressed Nora's spirits further, thanks to her assessment of Maggie's condition when she'd visited her in the hospital on her way in from the airport.

"We asked you to come home from New York and brainstorm with us because we haven't a clue," said Darien at last, clean-scrubbed and somewhat plain-looking in the tan skirt and blouse she'd worn beneath her white physician's coat during her shift in the same hospital's emergency room, where she was completing an internship. "That is, if you discount Steph's idea…"

It seemed Darien already had. "What *is* your idea, Steph?" Nora asked, bracing herself.

A successful, somewhat unconventional artist who played the stock market and lived with her latest boyfriend in a log cabin, twenty-three-year-old Stephanie was adept at concocting a plan for every situation. Unfortunately, to Nora's way of thinking, some of her past solutions had been downright foolish.

"Quite a hunk, isn't he?" Stephanie replied nonchalantly, tucking her stocking feet beneath her ankle-length, corduroy skirt. "You know, Nora, with your sexy good looks and fashion-model glamour, you might be able to fix things with him. You could wangle an introduction. Sweet-talk him into backing off...explain that, if he doesn't, Aunt Maggie will die. That she's been like a mother to you..."

Nora could feel Darien not-quite-looking at her. Something about her older sister's aversion to what had been said made her suspicious.

"Why me?" she demanded of Stephanie. "What makes you think he'd listen to me? Anyone named *Braet* is probably poison to him."

"He's known to prefer Western women...especially alluring, trophy women like you. I'll bet you could wrap him around your little finger. His hurt pride would be assuaged...."

Nora blushed. "You mean go to bed with him, don't you?" she said. "I know...you think I'm *so* old-fashioned. But I don't believe in sex outside of marriage. For your information, I'm still a virgin."

"At *twenty-five?*" Stephanie hooted. "That's a likely story."

"It happens to be the truth."

Darien winced at the exchange. "Stephanie...Nora...*please!*" she interposed. "Arguing isn't going to solve anything. Surely we can come up with some other approach."

Unfortunately, despite an additional hour of active brainstorming, they didn't manage to do so. Meanwhile, Nora had to fly back to New York the following morning. She was needed there to help prepare for the Evelyn Montoya fall showing, in which she was destined to play a starring role.

"I'm going back to the hospital," she said decisively, getting to her feet. "I want to spend as much time with Aunt Maggie as possible before I have to go." Her gaze softened as it rested on Darien. "We can talk by phone this evening," she told her older sister. "Or set up a conference call sometime later this week."

As she entered her aunt's small, private room with its adjustable hospital bed and IV stand hung with several plastic pouches that were slowly releasing their fluid contents into a vein on the back of Maggie Braet's left hand, Nora's heart broke. It was almost unbearable to see her beloved aunt looking so wan and thin against her pillow.

Clearly the chemotherapy was making her nauseous. Her nurse had placed a blue plastic basin within reach. The noxious chemicals that were flowing into her veins seemed also to have given her complexion a grayish tinge in contrast to the bleached-white color of the pillowcase. Usually poufed in her trademark upsweep, à la Katharine Hepburn, her gray-streaked auburn hair hung limply about her face in a flattened, tangled state. Ever more deeply etched lines around her eyes and mouth whispered that pain hadn't been a stranger.

"Ah, Nora," Maggie said with pleasure, opening her watery blue eyes. "You came back. It's so good to see you, dear."

"It's good to see *you*," Nora replied firmly, sitting on the edge of the bed despite hospital regulations and

taking her aunt's free hand in hers. "I just wish you
were feeling better, that's all. The chemotherapy…"

"…is going to make me well," Maggie vowed, despite the unaccustomed hoarse, wispy quality of her
voice. "I'll be back in the saddle at Braet's before you
know it. Surely after all these years you realize I'm not
the sort of person to succumb to a blob of puny, con-
fused cancer cells!"

Efficacious as the chemotherapy might prove, and
notwithstanding Maggie's positive outlook, her bright,
indomitable spirit, Nora was scared to death. Having
to give up her number-one reason for living in a hostile
takeover will literally kill her if the cancer doesn't, she
thought. So what if I'm reluctant to approach Seiji
Amundsen? I have to *do* something about this.

Spending as much time as she could with Maggie
before she had to say good-night, Nora tossed and
turned in her aunt's apartment. She phoned Darien the
next morning from the airport. "I have no intention of
prostituting myself the way Stephanie seemed to suggest yesterday," she told her older sister in no uncer-
tain terms. "But we have to do something about the
threatened takeover. If we don't, Aunt Maggie will die.
I'm absolutely sure of it."

Darien's silence seemed a tacit form of agreement.

"According to the article in *Worldview*," Nora
added, "Seiji Amundsen is supposed to be in New
York this coming week, attending an important meeting. At the very least, I'll try to contact him…appeal
to the basic decency of his human nature."

Nora was thinking about Seiji, and how to go about
wangling an introduction to him as her plane lifted off
at 6:20 a.m. and began to gain altitude amid thick gray

clouds. There was a better-than-even chance that he'd refuse to see her, she guessed. And if he did agree to meet with her? She was far from sure how to make the most of it without putting her virtue on the line the way Stephanie had suggested.

Meanwhile, it was 11:20 p.m. in Kyoto. Relaxing and sipping a small cup of *sake* in a traditional Japanese wooden tub of warm water after having been assiduously soaped and scrubbed by one of his female household attendants, the object of Nora's speculation was unwinding from a long business day. Once the servant had gathered up her bucket and brushes and left the room with downcast eyes, padding softly on her stocking feet, he reached for the copy of an American fashion magazine an assistant had obtained for him in connection with a current project.

In it, there were several full-color photos of Nora Braet in what Seiji regarded as outrageously titillating, if tailored, spring outfits. One shot featured a chartreuse linen two-piece suit with a tight, short skirt that emphasized her ultralong legs. It had a fitted, one-button jacket that gaped open in front, revealing that she wore no blouse or bra beneath it. Partly visible, the curve of her average-size but luscious right breast became the photo's focal point, stealing his appreciative masculine gaze from her face and the designer's overpriced creation.

A three-piece, ivory outfit Nora paraded in another photo had a similar effect on him. The photographer had captured her in the act of removing her jacket to reveal a body hugging stretch-lace blouse. Beneath it, she was braless. Though its pattern of roses and leaves had been carefully positioned to cover her nipples—by the couturier? the fashion coordinator? or Nora herself, out of modesty?—her shadowy peaks were still faintly visible under the creamy lace.

Immersed in his herb-scented bathwater, Seiji could feel his masculinity stir, his desire for her quicken. I wonder what it would be like to ravish her white skin with kisses, tangle my fingers in her long, red hair as I enter her? he thought. Prostrate her to unimaginable pleasure in my embrace. Setting the magazine aside for a moment, he imagined himself making passionate, sustained love to her.

He would make love to her at some point, of course. That was a given—part of the revenge he sought for her family's treatment of his female relatives. And it would be glorious. Afterward, he'd walk away, leaving her to yearn for more of the same while he focused his considerable energy on dismantling Braet & Company, renaming and absorbing it into a Japanese department-store empire he planned to take international.

Her deadpan hauteur in the photographs, her suggestive but somehow inaccessible poses, whispered that she wouldn't be an easy mark. So did her auburn tresses, which he'd been told were natural. According to his friends who'd grown up in the West, redheads were feisty. Stubborn. Given his publicized intention of waging war against her family's longtime retail chain, she might reject him out-of-hand. Play extremely hard to get.

Let her, he thought. She's the enemy. No permanent relationship can ever develop between us. Winning will be that much sweeter if she fights me tooth and nail.

By the time he'd picked up the magazine again and pored over Nora's photographs one last time, it was almost midnight. Drying off and donning a traditional Japanese kimono, Seiji phoned his New York office and ordered his manager there to arrange an introduction.

"I don't care *how* you do it. Just do it!" he snapped when the man suggested that setting up a meeting might be difficult.

By then, Nora was about forty minutes into her flight, drinking black coffee and passing up scrambled eggs with sausage for a bran muffin and grapefruit sections. Ironically she and Seiji were linked in thought as she tried to decide how to meet and deal with him.

I have to admit I find him extremely attractive, even sexy, she admitted with a little frisson of anticipation, aware she'd need to be objective if she planned to win him over without falling into the trap Stephanie had suggested. In her innocence, of course, she didn't have a clue about his agenda for her. Or guess that he was, at that very moment, arranging an opportunity to beguile her face-to-face.

Chapter Two

"Nora! Turn around... Tony needs to adjust your makeup!"

Immersed in the behind-the-scenes chaos of mounting the first fall showing of the prestigious Evelyn Montoya Collection at one of New York's premier hotels, Nora did as she was told. With the ease of long practice, she held herself motionless as cosmetics maestro Antonio Vargas put the finishing touches to her blusher, mascara and bright fuchsia lipstick. Her eyelids barely flickered as he dusted on additional face powder so the klieg lights and flashing cameras wouldn't highlight inappropriately shiny contours.

She'd be the first to parade out onto the so-called models' catwalk, the relatively narrow, elevated runway that would take her deep into the crowd of fashion writers, television cameramen and wealthy Montoya patrons who were waiting for the show to begin. The audience's reaction to her and to the skimpy red, black-and-fuchsia bouclé suit she wore would set the tone for the entire showing. Everything about her had to trumpet pizzazz and perfection.

As always at such moments, her mind seemed to float above the backstage free-for-all, focusing only peripherally on the designer's rising tension, the hairstylist's case of jitters, the other models' high-strung chatter and almost palpable nervousness.

Though she'd spent some time earlier that day fretting over Seiji Amundsen's planned takeover of Braet & Company and unsuccessfully trying to contact someone at his New York office who could arrange a meeting with him, he and the challenge he posed to her aunt Maggie and the family business were now the furthest things from her thoughts. She had entered a state of being that was intuitive, flow-driven, as aloof and dreamlike as she would appear to her stunned, appreciative audience.

Her only personal participation in the furor of last-minute adjustments to her outfit was a surreptitious check of the Velcro strips she'd insisted the alterations woman attach to the jacket's lining and the "blouse" of skimpy, wide-mesh netting she wore beneath it. When she twirled with her jacket partly open, she didn't want the gesture to reveal too much.

When the makeup man was finished, she also checked the list of costume changes that hung from her rack to make sure all the outfits she needed would be ready and waiting in the proper order.

Abruptly it was time. "Line up, girls," the floor director commanded in a stage whisper as the hairstylist made last-minute adjustments to Nora's grunge-inspired coiffure. "Isabel's about to start…"

Isabel Klein, second-in-command to the designer as well as a former speech and drama coach who possessed a low, melodic voice and unflappable stage presence, always took the microphone at Montoya openings. It freed her boss to remain backstage where she felt more comfortable and in-control until it was time to appear at the show's conclusion to receive applause.

As Nora took her place at the head of the line, Isabel was greeting the audience and expounding on the collection's theme, "Latin Influence." A moment later, the taped music that had been arranged especially for the show burst into a swingy Brazilian rhythm. Taking her cue from the floor director, Nora strutted out, a full six feet two inches tall in her three-inch platform heels, and headed down the runway. She was keenly aware of the many *oohs* and *aahs* that arose from the crowd through to her, in the spotlight, it was just a sea of upturned faces.

To Seiji, who'd managed to snag a front-row seat thanks to one of his influential business contacts, she looked confident, sexy and aloof. Her walk had the loose, rhythmic flow of a thoroughbred mare's or that of a cultivated woman who could barely resist breaking into a rendition of the tango.

What he guessed was a deliberate clash between the rich auburn of her piled-up, somewhat spiky-looking hair and the deep reds and fuchsias of her costume only made her appear that much more dramatic and unconventional.

Unlike some of the waiflike professional models he'd met at parties in the U.S. and overseas, Nora was hot. Sexy to the marrow. Not to mention drop-dead gorgeous. Yet in a way that only intensified his eagerness to meet her, she seemed unattainable. He had a strong impression that she'd been graced by both independence and intelligence.

When she left the stage to be supplanted by other models wearing what the narrator termed "jazzy, big-city outfits," he felt as if all the sparkle had gone out of the swanky, uptown hotel. He found himself drumming his fingers impatiently on the arm of his chair as he awaited her ensuing passes in more glamorous, revealing outfits.

She didn't disappoint. A few minutes later, she was back, her hair and makeup exquisitely redone, clad in the first of what the narrator termed "special occasion dresses." This time, she imparted her personal élan to a short, body-hugging, electric blue number with a matching fringed cape. As he watched, she unfurled the cape to reveal a deeply cut square neckline that bared a good deal of cleavage.

In marked contrast to her slender waist and slim-but-curvy thighs, her bosom appeared surprisingly full— doubtless, Seiji thought, courtesy of one of those push-up bras that had caused such a stir in the fashion world several years earlier.

But if it *hadn't* been lifted artificially? Experiencing a stab of desire he'd have preferred to save for the intoxicating moments he planned to spend in her arms, he imagined himself easing the dress's bodice from her shoulders and coaxing her rosy nipples to taut arousal.

They'd never share anything deeper than a fling, of course. Instead they'd remain on opposite sides of a very high fence, members of the separate Braet clans that had been created by his grandfather's concupiscence.

In her humiliation, Nora probably would be furious with him when, after bedding her, he refused what were sure to be her entreaties that he let Braet & Company off the hook. It didn't occur to him that, as a glamorous model who'd been pursued by many men, she might not want him. Or be willing to prostitute herself for the company's sake.

It's nothing to me if we become enemies, he thought, his predatory gray eyes narrowing. Her seduction and the humiliation of having her family's department-store chain absorbed into my empire anyway will even the score at last. When I think of the disgrace my grandmother felt when her husband's other children refused to be introduced to her...my mother's corrosive sense of shame and loss at being disowned by half her relatives...

His awareness that Nora had phoned Amundsen International's New York office several times in hopes of arranging a meeting with him only gave his anticipated victory over her a sweeter taste. She'd set herself up for what would happen by phoning him, thus saving him the trouble of pursuing her. To her, his appearance at the Eveyln Montoya opening would seem a simple, generous response to her overture.

Sportswear came next, followed by breathtakingly brief swimwear intended for postholiday Caribbean cruises. Sooner than Seiji had expected, the models were parading in evening gowns. Again Nora led the pack, sinuous in a full-length, backless sheath of fire engine red jersey.

This time, her hair was flowing in luxuriant waves around her shoulders. When she faced away from the audience to do a turn at the end of the runway, she sensuously swept it up at the nape with her hands, the better to reveal the crisscross arrangement of multiple rhinestone straps that kept her gown from falling to her ankles.

The move bared her back in a plunging V that ter-

minated just above her buttocks. With her arms raised
that way, the side curves of her bosom were fully in
evidence. Letting her hair slide in slow motion through
her fingers until it once again lay curled around her
shoulders, she gave the audience a brilliant smile, as if
to say, "Isn't this fun?" Her applause intensified.

When the traditional bridesmaid costumes appeared
and Nora wasn't among the models displaying them,
Seiji began to wonder if she'd return to the stage.
Maybe she'd slipped away to keep another appointment before Karyn Zens could deliver his message.
Still, it was a midweek, evening showing. He doubted
she had a crosstown engagement. According to what
he'd learned from Karyn, she didn't have a current
boyfriend.

A moment later, he guessed the likely reason for her
absence. Instead of taking her place among the attendants at the show's finale, she'd be its star, glowing in
Evelyn Montoya's wedding dress like a Christmas angel.

Backstage, Nora's dresser was swearing under her
breath as she attempted to secure the low-cut, strapless
bodice of Nora's gown in place. Though it was touch
and go, Nora tried not to concern herself. Still, she
couldn't quite shake her worry that, if the woman
didn't get it right, there'd be startled gasps, a bit more
of her showing than Mrs. Montoya had intended.

Meanwhile, the hairstylist and his assistant were
rushing to complete the coiffure of multiple-looped
braids the designer had requested in time for Nora's
entrance.

Somehow it all fell into place, including the careful
placement of her veil and yet another adjustment to her
makeup, by the time Isabel Klein was ready to an-

nounce her entrance. Giving her an air kiss and a little push in the direction of the curtain, the floor director indicated her readiness.

She stepped into view at the appointed organ pulse of the wedding march, parting the waves of applause that met her appearance like some kind of ethereal apparition, or goddess. Seconds later, she put some sway into her step as the traditional chords segued into a rhumba beat. The applause was deafening.

If and when I get married someday, I'll have to step up to the altar in leggings and a sweatshirt just for the novelty of it, she thought, enjoying the mental image as she gave the crowd her most brilliant smile. To me, a traditional wedding gown will seem passé.

As she paraded toward him, Seiji all but held his breath. Her dress was strapless—fashioned of body-caressing white satin so slippery-looking it seemed to flow from just above the crest of her bosom down over her hips like a waterfall, trailing off into a minitrain that she handled easily.

A short, full veil of white tulle sprung from the sparkling pearl-and-zirconia encrusted pillbox that crowned her head, its bouffant width and cropped length in vivid contrast to the gown's long, liquid silhouette.

For the first time in his life, Seiji could understand the pride and humility with which some men claimed the woman of their choice in a wedding ceremony. If Nora were the bride, he guessed, those emotions wouldn't flow solely from possessing her. Instead they would arise from her willingness to give herself.

Such a joining could never happen between them, of course. To begin with, he wasn't in the market to marry anyone—certainly not the daughter and granddaughter of people who had treated his family so shabbily. Nor did he wish to fall in love with her, even on a temporary basis. His vow to exact a fitting punishment from the Braets precluded it.

Yet all wasn't lost by any means. Intuition whispered that she'd be a worthy opponent in the battle of wits and seduction he'd planned for them.

The show ended to wild applause. At the appropriate moment, Evelyn Montoya appeared in one of her own more conservative but festive designs, with the tiny, trademark glasses she usually wore perched on the bridge of her nose. She positively glowed at the praise being heaped on her efforts.

Nora remained onstage with the other models until the designer had completed her thank-yous, applauding for her and the long list of people she credited. At last the show was officially over. She could retreat.

Quickly unbraided and brushed, her hair ended in a mass of waves and ringlets. She was in the act of changing from the wedding gown she'd worn into the leggings, tank top and oversize sweatshirt she'd been thinking about earlier when her agent appeared.

"Karyn…what on earth are you doing here?" she asked. "I thought you had other plans this evening."

"I had to cancel them." Nora's petite, perpetually wired-on-caffeine agent didn't offer any details. "You were marvelous tonight, as always," she said. "Listen…I need you to do me a favor. There's somebody in the audience…a man…who wants to make your acquaintance."

Nora rolled her eyes. "Isn't there always?"

Karyn shook her head. "This one's different. Besides, I owe a friend of his. You'd be doing it for my sake."

Nora pictured a pudgy, self-important executive with six pairs of hands and an underappreciated wife in Westchester County. Making small talk with such a person instead of going home to a well-earned TV dinner and the mystery thriller she'd almost finished reading was the very last thing she wanted.

Still, Karyn seemed serious about her indebtedness. A pushover for friends in need, Nora agreed to say hello for her agent's sake. "C'mon," she said, slinging her backpack over one shoulder. "Let's get it over with."

"Not like that!" Karyn shrieked. "Can't you at least borrow a *dress?*"

A backless black jersey sheath with a bateau neckline in front and appropriate shoes in Nora's size were quickly rounded up.

"Thanks, Isabel…I'll return them as soon as I can…hopefully in a few minutes," Nora promised. "Hang onto my backpack for me, okay?"

There were still quite a few people milling around in the ballroom though the bulk of the crowd gradually was making its way to the exits. Following Karyn down the narrow aisle between the left side of the runway and the first row of chairs, Nora kept pausing to respond to starry-eyed compliments. She signed several autographs, one of them for a gangly twelve-year-old who hoped to be in her shoes someday. Thus distracted, she was totally unprepared for her unknown admirer's identity until her agent brought them face-to-face.

It can't *be.* I must be imagining this, she thought in amazement, gazing into narrowed eyes the color of storm clouds at sea—eyes she'd first met on the pages of a magazine. Yet there wasn't any doubt. The man who'd asked to meet her was Seiji Amundsen. She'd tried so hard to get in touch with him and batted zero. Now Karyn was handing him to her on a plate.

He was roughly an inch taller than she despite her three-inch, black suede heels, making him six foot three or thereabouts. And so good-looking she realized his photograph hadn't begun to do him justice. His mouth's slight curve and the little "quote-mark" indentations that framed it hinted at stubbornness and sensuality. He appeared to have a light suntan on skin that was only marginally darker than her fair Titian complexion. His dark brown hair glowed like the pelt of a healthy animal.

Everything about him, from the lift of his brows to his snowy shirt cuffs, radiated confidence and sex appeal. She suppressed a shiver at the way he ran his eyes over her from head to toe before returning them to her face. Abruptly it occurred to her that she'd been guilty of a similar transgression.

A bit nervously, as if she sensed the crackle of erotic energy that excluded her, Karyn introduced them.

He bowed.

"Hello," Nora said, catching a whiff of the subtle but provocative aftershave he wore as he took her hand.

His fingers were strong and warm as they sheltered hers. "It's a pleasure to meet you, Miss Braet," he answered, the quote marks deepening as if from some secret satisfaction. "We're distant relatives, you know."

She wanted to say something offhand and casual—prove to him and her manager that she wasn't vulnerable to his considerable allure. "Yes, I did know that," she admitted.

He continued to hold her hand. She could feel Karyn

staring at her, surprised she'd allow a stranger to pro-
long the physical contact.

Gently withdrawing her fingers, she turned to her
agent. "My great-grandfather was Mr. Amundsen's
grandfather," she explained. "He married twice. According to my grandmother, who specialized in ge-
neaology, that makes us half cousins once removed.
None of us have ever met our Japanese relations."

From Seiji's viewpoint, she'd cut to the heart of the
matter with breathtaking clarity while placing him
firmly in what she doubtless considered his most appropriate ethnic category. "Of course, that's been rem-
edied now," he said smoothly, keeping his skepticism
of her fairness under wraps.

After several minutes of banter awash in cross currents, he asked Nora and Karyn if they were free to
join him for a late supper. He was a bachelor, a visitor
in New York. He'd appreciate the company.

Clearly aware he was interested in Nora, not her, and
unwilling to be a fifth wheel on the bandwagon of his
pursuit, Karyn replied that she had other plans. She
gave Nora a pleading look.

Still contemplating Seiji with a view to discussing
Braet & Company's fate while trying to put the brakes
on her fascination with him, Nora didn't answer for a
moment. She soundly rejected the notion that he'd have
trouble finding a date.

"I suppose *I* could go," she said at last. "That is,
if you're willing to drop me at my apartment building
afterward."

The handsome grandson of her great-grandfather replied that it would be his pleasure to do so.

"I'll need to fetch my, er, purse," Nora murmured,
taking a backward step.

She brushed off Karyn's thanks as, once again, they dove into the backstage fracas of sorting and packing the designer's gowns for their return trip to her showroom. "Actually I've been trying to reach him for reasons of my own," she acknowledged. "You did *me* a favor. Hey, Isabel...could you keep my backpack for me overnight? And lend me an evening purse?"

Having transferred her wallet, keys and a lipstick to the tiny moiré bag with a rhinestone shoulder strap Evelyn Montoya's first assistant had handed her with a smile, Nora accepted the loan of a matching ruana as well, and returned to the ballroom. Except for Seiji, the hotel cleanup crew and a few die-hard members of the audience who were chatting in little groups, it was mostly empty.

When she reached him, he didn't speak. Instead he offered her his arm, gave her one of his enigmatic smiles and steered her toward the exit.

His limousine was waiting at the curb.

Tipping his cap to her without any sign of curiosity or even interest, the uniformed Japanese driver shut the door for them and got behind the wheel. A few seconds later, they were caught up in the steady stream of taillights and oncoming vehicles that epitomized city traffic.

They were seated in fairly close proximity and again Nora caught the elusive aroma of Seiji's aftershave. This time, it mingled with his natural skin scent. Without appearing to do so, she drank it deeply into her nostrils. She could hardly believe they were in a taxi, heading off into the night together.

"Where are we going?" she asked.

"Somewhere we can dance," he answered firmly. "Do you have a preference?"

She shook her head.

Sliding open the window that separated them from the driver, he uttered a few words in Japanese along with the name of a five-star hotel on the upper East Side. In addition to a truly marvelous French restaurant, it had an intimate little cabaret with live music and a vest-pocket dance floor.

When he relaxed against the seat beside Nora again, his knee was positioned lightly against hers. *I didn't bargain for this kind of intimacy,* she thought with a little frisson of attraction that curled her toes. *It hints at seduction—of* me *by him, not the other way around, as Stephanie had the effrontery to suggest.*

It occurred to her that he might be planning to add her to his list of conquests, along with Braet & Company, as a kind of trophy in his war against her family. If that was the plan, she'd better make her pitch to him, and quickly. Still, it seemed best to do it over dinner, after they'd gotten to know each other a little better. She would wait for the right opening.

Meanwhile, the silence between them in the limousine was deafening. She had to say something, if only to ease the tension a little. "You don't exactly look Japanese…" she blurted, wishing instantly that she'd kept her mouth shut or come up with something a lot more tactful.

His reply was smooth, if a little prickly. "As you've probably heard," he said in his rich baritone, "I'm something of a mongrel."

The term was harshly self-deprecating. She wasn't sure how to respond to it. To her relief, it seemed no overt offense had been taken as he helped her out of the limousine at their destination and guided her inside, through the hotel's sparkling marble, crystal and mahogany lobby to its renowned French restaurant, Le Verger des Pêches.

At that hour on a weekday night, the place wasn't crowded. Though Nora knew it had recently undergone refurbishing, this was the first time she'd had a chance to see the results. She hadn't bargained for the lush, erotic effect of extensive, larger-than-life murals featuring a postmodernist's all-female rendering of *Déjeuner sur l'Herbe,* with buxom, serene-looking nudes lounging on the grass in a peach orchard. The women's hair, their velvety skin and rosy nipples, had been rendered in the soft, rich hues of ripening peaches.

It's obvious they're daydreaming about their lovers, she thought, then blushed at her private interpretation of the artist's concept as she turned her attention to intimate, dark green velvet banquettes, gilt-framed mirrors adorned with cupids, the ornate crystal chandeliers that were reflected in them. The management had chosen peach-colored tablecloths and napkins that reproduced the mural's tones of sun-warmed flesh. What few sharp edges the restaurant possessed were softened by candlelight. The effect was utterly private and sensuous.

It turned out the maître d' was expecting them.

"Does my choice of restaurant suit you?" Seiji inquired, in a low tone as the man escorted them to a table.

A little shiver of excitement slid down Nora's spine as she made eye contact with him. "It's charming," she answered with the faultless composure she'd learned to use as a model, no matter how disarmed or flustered she might be feeling. "If I'm staring, that's because the place has been redone recently. This is my first chance to see the new decor..."

Their waiter appeared just moments after they were seated. Ordering champagne, Seiji decided that—the testimony of her slim figure to the contrary—she probably knew the interiors of New York's best-known watering holes firsthand. A legion of handsome, wealthy admirers were doubtless falling all over themselves in their eagerness to take her wherever she wanted to go.

At Seiji's suggestion, they drank a toast to more closely knit family relationships after their champagne was uncorked. Nora wasn't sure what he meant by that, though she could guess. For several seconds, the awkward topic of her family's treatment of his grandmother and mother seemed to hover almost tangibly in the air between them. She wondered how on earth she was going to approach him about Braet & Company if, as she suspected, he was nursing a substantial grudge on their behalf.

Things went a little better over their meal of *Coquilles St. Jacques* and *Sole à la Normande* with shrimp, cider and Portobello mushrooms as Seiji questioned her about her work and answered her queries about his international travel and far-flung enterprises.

Still, a smoldering undercurrent of attraction, together with the strong feeling that they were adversaries in a subliminal chess game of his making, continued to keep her off balance. When their fingers brushed as they exchanged portions of their desserts, she realized abruptly that he felt it, too, the same unnerving sense of opposition and arousal.

They didn't talk much as they switched to the adjoining cabaret, where a pianist and a trumpet player were providing smooth, dance-quality jazz from the forties and fifties. Seiji ordered after-dinner drinks, sake for him and a cognac for her. Seconds later, he was inviting her to join him on the dance floor. When he held out his arms, she stepped into them like a woman hypnotized, drinking his wonderful, difficult-to-define scent into her nostrils.

The sensation of being held in such close proximity to this extraordinary man she'd heard about for years and finally met was like nothing she'd ever experienced—sweeter by far than the apricot *jalousie* and miniature rum baba they'd sampled together. Both tall and long-legged though she owed part of her height to three-inch heels and he was more muscular than she, they meshed to perfection. It was as if, an ocean apart with steep cultural and familial divides separating them, they'd been born to partner each other.

I don't want to feel this way about him, Nora protested to herself. It'll unhinge all my plans...put me at a strong disadvantage in my effort to win the concessions Aunt Maggie needs. Besides, nothing can possibly come of it. To her dismay, when he rested his cheek against her hair, she couldn't seem to stop herself from nestling closer, the better to feel the hard masculine outline of his body against hers.

Usually quite calculating and independent in his dealings with women, Seiji, too, was carried away by the moment. He found it far too easy to imagine them naked atop tangled sheets as he pumped the seed of his exotic, summarily disowned heritage into her body.

They'd have to use protection, of course. Anything less would be irresponsible. Yet he had to admit he was turned on by the sweet if vengeful notion of getting her pregnant. He didn't have the slightest doubt they'd make a beautiful child together.

The burgeoning of his manhood against her thigh and the agitation it prompted caused Nora to drop her purse. Pausing in midbeat, Seiji reached down and picked it up, blatantly sliding the hand that had collected it up her smooth, nylon-encased leg before replacing its strap on her shoulder. Her eyes were huge, their dilated pupils all but swallowing the green of her irises as, with a little sigh of satisfaction, he gathered her close.

At last he offered to see her home. She felt a moment's panic as she gathered her borrowed ruana and arranged it around her shoulders, afraid she'd blown her opportunity to speak to him about Braet & Company. Despite the likelihood that he'd take it for a proposal of another sort, she'd have to invite him up to her apartment for coffee or an aperitif, broach the topic of his intended takeover while she still had the chance.

Her building was just a few blocks away. During the short ride over, his left arm lightly encircled her shoulders as if to state a transitory possessiveness. She hoped he couldn't sense the way she was fretting about how to approach him.

"Would you like to come up for a minute?" she asked casually when they pulled to the curb, as if the idea had just occurred to her. "I can fix some coffee. Or..."

She was about to make her pitch. Having expected it from the beginning, Seiji didn't have the slightest difficulty guessing what her invitation was about. Despite the instinctive way she'd responded to him on the dance floor in the little cabaret, he didn't delude himself that she wanted to have sex with him. Or that she was interested in him as a person. Though the attraction was there, he sensed, she'd consider him beyond the pale.

"I suppose I could come up for a few minutes," he answered slowly. "Unfortunately I can't stay long. I have an early meeting."

They didn't exchange many words as they went up together in her building's brass-and-walnut elevator. Or as she unlocked her apartment door. The reason for his quiet, composed air wasn't clear to her. As for her silence, it was filled to the brim by last-minute conjecture about how to approach him on behalf of her family's department-store chain.

First she'd fix him the libation of his choice, she decided. When it was ready, she'd sit him down in one of her ultra-comfortable tub chairs by the windows and talk to him about her aunt Maggie's illness, explain how much it saddened and worried her.

If he expressed sympathy—the polite thing for anyone to do, especially someone raised in the ultra-courteous Japanese tradition, she'd explain how much the business meant to Maggie and beg him not to steal it from her in a hostile takeover. Perhaps some form of accommodation could be worked out. It went without saying that she'd have to apologize profusely for the way her branch of the family had treated his, become a lightning rod for his displeasure before he'd even consider her request.

Nora never made it to the kitchen. Or her liquor cabinet. Just inside her front door, which he'd shut firmly behind them so that the lock clicked into place, he placed his hands on her shoulders. She could feel their heat through her borrowed dress, predict the conflagration his mouth would touch off as he bent his head to hers.

Like kindling in the path of a forest fire, she was devoured by his kiss, consumed by its almost preternatural radiance. It was as if they'd been fated to join that way since he'd turned nine and she'd been a chubby, redheaded infant. Maybe even before their respective births. Everything he had, everything he was, she drank into herself. Everything she knew how to give was his for the taking. All he had to do was reach for it.

With a little sigh of surprise and pleasure, he gathered her closer and thrust his tongue into her mouth. What a delectable woman she was! Her nipples were pebbles of arousal against his chest as he drew her closer. His hands cupped her buttocks, drawing her lower body against his response, so that she could assess his readiness.

Lacking a firebreak, some effective means of defending herself from what she suddenly wanted more than anything else on earth, Nora realized what a concession she'd be making. She'd offer herself, the innocence she'd struggled to preserve for the man she'd marry someday. And get nothing in return. Aunt Maggie's cause would flounder in the breach.

I've got to put a stop to this, she thought half coherently. Tell him what's on my mind and beg him to be merciful. Apologize like crazy for my family's treatment of his relatives…

To her surprise and dismay, he chose that precise moment to draw back first.

Glittering with the arousal he felt but didn't plan to pursue that evening, Seiji's eyes appeared to seek out her vulnerability and find it. "Sorry but I'll have to pass on the drink," he announced after a moment. "It's getting late. I need to awaken refreshed."

"Whereas I have an 8:00 a.m. photo session with one of the major magazines," she answered defensively before she could stop herself.

His mouth curving slightly as if he'd expected that kind of response—maybe even elicited it, he shrugged and replied with a casual American metaphor, "Then we're in the same boat."

If I let him leave without broaching the topic of Braet & Company, I might not have another chance, Nora thought. There was also the disconcerting fact that she wanted to see him again for his own sake. "How long do you plan to be in New York?" she blurted.

The words seemed to tilt the balance of power between them in his direction. Though his storm-hued gaze didn't waver, it acknowledged the shift. "Until the middle of next week," he answered finally. "Will it be possible for us to see each other again?"

A little tingle of anticipation came to rest between her legs. She nodded.

"I'll call you, then."

His promise was no guarantee. Still, Nora was relieved all out of proportion to the mission she'd agreed to undertake. She snatched up a piece of scrap of paper from her entry-hall desk and wrote down the digits of her private cell-phone number.

"You can reach me at this number anytime," she whispered.

Chapter Three

There wasn't any doubt in Nora's mind as she stripped off her makeup and got into the shower. Seiji Amundsen had wanted to make love to her. And, despite her strong intention of remaining a virgin until her wedding day, she'd wanted to let him. Desire had descended like a ton of bricks, plunging her into a free fall of passion she'd only dreamed about.

Soaping her body beneath the spray, an activity that was usually perfunctory if pleasurable, spun out her heightened awareness to the point that she could think of nothing but the yearning he'd evoked. We've just met, for God's sake! she thought. We've known each other for a couple of hours, at best. And he's threatening Maggie with the loss of Braet & Company. What on earth can I be thinking about?

More to the point were her distant cousin's reasons for looking her up in response to her phone messages. Given his reputation as a shark in business dealings, he might just as easily have played it cool, let her come begging on her knees to him.

Why hadn't he?

It struck her that his appearance at the Evelyn Montoya opening that evening might have been a calculated one—the introductory gambit in a scheme to bed her as part of any deal he was willing to strike. Supposedly he was Machiavellian enough to use whatever means happened to be at hand to attain his ends. If he was bent on punishing and humiliating her family by deflowering and discarding her, he'd certainly achieve his purpose.

He could use the company as bait.

A moment later, she was shaking her head. The idea was just too preposterous. Civilized people didn't behave that way. And he was nothing if not civilized, despite his predatory air.

Drying off with one of the thick, oversize towels she favored renewed the heightened awareness his kiss had provoked. About to reach for her nightgown, which hung from a hook on the back of the bathroom door, she stayed her hand. For once, she decided, she'd slip naked into bed. Something about the way Seiji had kissed her made her long to feel the cool, smooth texture of the sheets against her body.

The moment I shut my eyes, I can see his face, she acknowledged, rearranging her pillows and switching off her bedside lamp. Those vaguely exotic, smoke-colored eyes. That aquiline nose. Those emphatic brows. To her discredit, she was thoroughly charmed by the way his sensuous, mobile mouth was framed by expressive, slightly amused parentheses.

She didn't doubt he could look closed and arrogant. Be utterly unapproachable. She just hadn't seen those incarnations yet. Meanwhile, his controlled intensity was an overpowering force. The impassioned female she was in her secret heart cast him as a modern-day samurai warrior who'd ably assumed the role of corporate raider and international businessman. It was all too likely she'd be outclassed in any negotiations she might attempt with him.

Assailed by guilt for not bringing up Maggie's illness and her dependence on Braet & Company for a reason to live, Nora wondered if her handsome adversary would actually call the scribbled phone number she'd given him. It was all too likely he'd crumple it up and toss it into the wastebasket when he reached his hotel room. If he returned to Japan without getting in touch, she'd have a hard time explaining to Stephanie and Darien why she'd spent the better part of an evening in his company without so much as mentioning their aunt's ill health and the family department-store chain.

She was at the point of drifting into disconnected dreams when the phone on her night table shrilled. "Hello?" she answered sleepily on the second ring.

Stretched out in his shorts atop the king-size bed that dominated the sleeping area of his luxurious hotel suite, Seiji tormented himself with her imagined state of undress. She had such long, shapely legs. And tempting breasts. In the all-but-backless white swimsuit she'd modeled earlier that evening, her buttocks had been sheer perfection.

As for the unique, as yet unknown person she was inside her satin skin, he sensed a worthy opponent. The air of untrammelled innocence she projected—an illusion, surely, concocted to confuse him—would only lend zest to his pursuit.

"I didn't wake you, did I?" he asked.

It was Seiji. The realization took hold. "Not entirely," she admitted. "I was in that halfway state where reality stumbles into imagining."

She wasn't just beautiful. She was also bright and articulate. Surrounded by the lavish but unimaginative elegance of his five-star hotel suite, Seiji wished he'd let desire, rather than the exigencies of his plan to exact revenge upon her, rule their earlier interchange. If he had, he might have been in bed with her at that very moment.

"You're too generous," he allowed. "However, now that you're awake, I may as well tell you what I called about. I've been invited to spend the weekend with some friends on Martha's Vineyard and I wondered if you'd like to join me. We could spend our time on the island getting to know each other."

She accepted, of course, though it meant canceling an important photo session. In view of the concession she needed from him, she didn't have any other choice. Yet as she lay awake thinking about the way his kiss had tasted for almost an hour after returning the receiver to its cradle, she was forced to admit that saving Braet's was far from her only reason for agreeing to see him again.

You can't afford to feel so *heated* about him, she warned herself, snuggling beneath the covers. Or imagine something real happening between you when so many barriers stand in the way.

Even without the breach her great-grandfather's scandalous behavior had caused, they hailed from different worlds...disparate spheres of custom and outlook that didn't plait easily with each other. Besides, it was like she'd told Stephanie. She wasn't the kind of woman to settle for a hit-and-run affair. Everything about his track record shrieked that his heart was out of reach.

Friday dawned a perfect mid-September day—bright, unseasonably warm and breezy. Nora dressed for their trip in a blue-and-white striped knit top with a coordinating solid blue cardigan and miniskirt, her darkest sunglasses. As arranged, Seiji picked her up shortly after 9:00 a.m. in his chauffeur-driven limousine. Greeting her at her door with an unnerving light kiss instead of the traditional Japanese bow, he carried her bags down in the elevator, handing them over to his driver when they reached the sidewalk.

With a little sigh of incredulity at the situation in which she found herself, Nora got inside and settled back against the plush upholstery for the four-plus-hour drive via Interstate 95 to Woods Hole, Massachusetts, and the car ferry dock. Seiji quickly took his place beside her, and they were on their way. He had chosen to sit in close proximity to her and, when he pressed a button, causing a console to open in front of them, his sleeve grazed hers.

Along with the usual stash of liquor most private limousines carried, the console contained a steaming pot of Japanese green tea and carafe of piping hot American coffee. Courteously Seiji poured Nora's choice of tea and handed it to her in an oriental-style ceramic cup.

"Here's the *Times* if you're interested," he said, offering her the morning paper. "I hope you won't mind if I use part of our travel time to go over some contracts. It's the price of getting out of town and spending a weekend with you."

Nora shook her head.

What else can I say? she added silently. That I want to talk to you about Braet & Company and my aunt's illness...*now*, without wasting another second? You probably know that anyway. Much as I'd like to get my plea on Aunt Maggie's behalf off my chest, it would hardly be the most effective way of reaching you.

The tea had a pleasantly woodsy, almost botanical taste. Self-consciously keeping her thigh separate from his without noticeably seeming to inch away from him, she buried herself in the paper, starting with the front section. It wasn't until she reached the business pages that she spotted a piece on Amundsen International's likely takeover of Braet & Company. According to the journalist who'd written it, Seiji had amassed an estimated thirty-eight percent of the chain's outstanding shares.

A little shiver passed through her. It was even worse than they'd thought. He'd handed her the paper for the sole purpose of rubbing her nose in it!

A quick, upward glance on her part surprised an expression of pride and something more difficult to define on his face.

"How intriguing...a beautiful woman who bothers to read the business pages," he commented, an ironic little smile playing at the corners of his mouth. "Yes, I know. There's a piece on Braet & Company you probably want to discuss with me. I'll be happy to oblige at some point. Meanwhile, what do you say we spend a little time just enjoying the weekend and getting to know each other?"

It was what she wanted, too, though she felt guilty

at the delay. "Okay," she agreed. "But you're right. I *do* want to talk to you about Braet & Company."

Giving her a look that said he admired her frankness, Seiji slipped the contracts he'd been going over back into his briefcase and poured more tea for them. As they continued to drive northeast, he initiated a casual conversation that focused on their respective growing-up years.

A hint of nostalgia creeping into his tone, he spoke of taking part in a formal moon viewing for the first time as a child of four, the many presents and colorful banners he'd received on Boys' Day, an annual Japanese celebration. His eyes shone as he described his excitement over learning the finer points of falconry at the country home of his mother's great-uncle.

"When I was nine, my father took us to Denmark for the first time," he said. "I was astonished by the way people lived, the food they ate. It was my first taste of what life could be like on an international scale."

Questions from him drew forth memories of Nora picking blackberries on her grandmother's farm as a child of eight, her flair for dressing up in fashion leftovers from Braet & Company provided by her aunt Maggie.

She almost stumbled and told him about her father's unhappy proclivity for cheating on his subsequent spouses following her mother's early death. Instead she mentioned being first runner-up to the homecoming queen at the high school she'd attended despite what she described as her terminal shyness, the fact she'd represented her classmates in a Latin tournament.

"Why didn't you do something with your aptitude

for languages?'' he asked. "Did you find it boring compared to modeling?''

Nora shrugged. "Not at all. Just different. Modeling pays a lot better than working as a translator when you're fortunate enough to land at the top of the heap. Maybe I'll become a linguist when I retire someday. That's what I trained for at UW.''

His thigh pressed against hers as he leaned a little closer, sending a tremor of awareness rippling through her body. "What languages did you study?'' he asked softly in his rough-edged baritone.

Nora moved an equal distance away from him without making a production of it. "Mostly French and Spanish, with a little German thrown in,'' she said.

"Any Japanese?''

She shook her head. "Since Jerrold's defection, no one in our branch of the family has visited Japan or even considered going there. I didn't think it would have much practical application.''

On the forty-five-minute ferry trip from Cape Cod to the island of Martha's Vineyard, they stood together at the rail, Nora's hair only partially prevented from whipping in the breeze by a silk-print scarf as Seiji sheltered her with an arm around her shoulders. Despite the salt tang of the air, she couldn't help but be aware of his aftershave, an offbeat, hard-to-place blend that suited his exotic background to perfection.

Back in the limousine, they drove off the ferry ramp at Oak Bluffs, a quaint New England-style village full of specialty restaurants, touristy little shops and National Register houses, and headed south toward the area known as West Tisbury, which faced Vineyard Sound. Some of them owned by famous people, the mansions that fronted on the water were partly hidden at the end of long, winding driveways.

Before long, they were turning in at a pair of wooden gateposts. The landscape left little doubt that they were approaching the ocean. Beyond the wind-bent, stunted trees that lined the unpaved driveway, a sprawling, shingle-style house beckoned from its grassy knoll overlooking the water.

"The McEwens are business associates," Seiji remarked as they drew up to its front door. "This is party weekend, I'm told. We won't be the only guests."

Their hostess, Pam McEwen, a slim blond woman with patrician features and an air of old money, welcomed them enthusiastically. "You made it in time to go fishing!" she exclaimed, giving Seiji a hug and pumping Nora's hand when he introduced them. "Everyone's down at the marina already. I'll phone and let them know we're coming...have one of the servants carry your things upstairs so you can change."

To Nora's relief, the house was huge; she and Seiji had been assigned separate bedrooms. As soon as her luggage arrived, she substituted white duck trousers for her miniskirt and nylons, slid her feet into white deck shoes and added a dab of lipstick.

Seiji was attired in light-colored trousers and a black, short-sleeve T-shirt that bared his muscular arms when they met again in the upstairs hall. Anticipating a stiff breeze, he'd knotted a cabled black cotton pullover around his shoulders. The dark-colored garments so close to his face brought out his hair's tawny lights.

The McEwen's power yacht, which boasted a tuna tower above its flying bridge, was berthed at Menemsha. They and their hostess were the last to come aboard. Even before they'd been served drinks by the cabin boy, several of their fellow guests had cast off the moorings, visibly eager to be under way. Their host, Charlie McEwen, who grinned and waved to them from the bridge, quickly maneuvered his craft out into the channel.

Picking up the minute they hit open water, the breeze played havoc with Nora's hair, all but obscuring her vision. To make matters worse, she'd forgotten her scarf. She could sense the other women in their party taking her measure as Seiji gently turned her away from him to plait her hair into a thick, medium-length braid.

The experience was a sensual one for them both. Nora found herself suffering internal quivers of delight she hoped weren't reflected in her expression. As for Seiji, the fact that she'd let him touch her in that casual but affectionate way in front of strangers wove a cocoon of intimacy around them that he was eager to explore.

He decided to push the envelope. "I'm sure you realize that sunlight reflects off the water, doubling the dose of ultraviolet rays your skin absorbs," he reminded. "Given the fairness of your complexion, you ought to wear sunblock. I happened to bring a tube along. If you haven't done so yet, I'll put some on your face and hands, the back of your neck. And you can return the favor."

It was another excuse to touch her, have her touch him. And she realized it. But she didn't object. Her only negative emotion was one of frustration that her engrossment with him had caused her to forget the protective measures she usually took against sunburn.

The ongoing contact only added fuel to the fire of their attraction. He feels it, too, she thought. Even if evoking it is calculated on his part. With every glance, every touch, she was being knitted more irrevocably into a web of longing that would demand to be satisfied.

She got a breather from the stress of it when they slowed in the area where some fellow anglers had reported over their craft's radio that the tuna were running.

"They're talking about *bluefin* tuna," Seiji told her as the fishing gear was handed out. "They can weigh up to seven hundred pounds, you know. An unbruised fish that size would be worth approximately $14,000 in Tokyo, where it would be served in sparing portions at the city's sushi bars."

The waters off Martha's Vineyard also held swordfish, sea bass, cod, sturgeon and hake. Since no license was required for ocean fishing, Nora and Seiji were free to try their luck.

Helping her bait her hook and cast her line into the diamond-bright water, Seiji moved a short distance away and baited his own hook. The other guests, three men and two women, did likewise. Pam McEwen joined her husband on the bridge as they began to troll, looking for likely prospects.

It was beginner's luck, as she'd never been deep-sea fishing before, Nora would argue later, causing her fellow guests to roll their eyes and give her disbelieving looks. Whatever their opinion of her claim, some twenty minutes later she hooked into a smallish bluefin and watched her line unreel with dizzying speed into the water's depths.

"Hold him! Don't let him take it all or you'll have nothing left to fight him with!" Seiji shouted, dropping his own gear and racing to stand behind her so he could fasten a fighting harness around her to protect her back from injury. "That's it...put on the drag and hold steady. Let him know who's boss."

A battle royal, her struggle with the fish seemed to last forever. To her dismay, he sounded several times. Standing behind her, Seiji instructed her what to do from moment to moment. As she fought the wild ocean creature to which she'd attached herself and finally hauled it into the boat, she didn't lose her keen awareness of him, a man similarly undomesticated, pressing his body to hers as he helped with the daunting task.

The sparks that seemed destined to fly between them were undiminished as someone snapped a picture of them with her catch.

"Well done," he whispered, leaning toward her for the benefit of the photograph. "You have the makings of a pro."

Her response was muted and he found himself puzzling over it. A moment later, the reason became clear.

"Here...let me take this fellow off your hands and put him on ice for you," one of the other men offered. "You can have a taxidermist fix him up and hang him over your fireplace."

She surprised everyone when she answered that she didn't want to keep her catch. "Please...take the hook out of his mouth and throw him back in the water," she said.

"In line with my earlier calculations, this fish is worth roughly $2,200," Seiji reminded. "Though that's retail in Japan, you'd still have the price of a designer dress."

On sale, if I were lucky, she countered silently. *It wouldn't be worth it.* She shook her head. "Money isn't everything. And I have enough dresses. I want to put him back in the ocean while he's still alive and beautiful.''

Returning to shore some three hours later, after several other members of their party had landed fish as well, they were transported back to the house, where they stretched out to rest in their separate rooms. They met again around 6:30 p.m. when Nora came down their hosts' central staircase. Seiji was waiting for her in a Brooks Brothers jacket, silk tie and neatly pressed linen trousers.

For the buffet-style dinner, which would be held outdoors on the terrace thanks to the unseasonably warm weather and the flagging breeze off the water, Nora had chosen a simple flowered dress with long sleeves and a short, flippy skirt.

"You look lovely," Seiji said in an undertone, offering her his arm. "But you were right...you have enough dresses. I'd rather see you in a swimming suit like the one you modeled at the Montoya opening."

She was still flushed from the compliment when they joined the McEwens and their other guests, to sip champagne and toast each other's fishing prowess.

I can't afford to be so strongly affected by him, she reminded herself as one of the other women engaged her in conversation. Still, though she barely knew him, he was her closest ally in a houseful of strangers. Maybe holding onto that thought would help her muster the courage to tackle their discussion about Braet & Company without waiting for an invitation.

On Monday morning, he'd said, he'd be flying to Vancouver. And after that, Kyoto. She might not have another chance. Unfortunately something excited and helpless in her kept urging her to put off confronting him a little longer and see what developed.

Several of the McEwens' island neighbors joined them in time for the meal. There was some storytelling over dessert by one of the houseguests, obviously a longtime business associate of Seiji's, which offered Nora a little more insight into his character as it pertained to his negotiating methods. The tales didn't bode particularly well for her success with him. But they did increase her desire to get their confrontation over with. If he agreed to be merciful, who knew what might develop.

After dinner, their host plugged a CD player into one of the terrace outlets and put on some dance music. Though the air was getting chillier as the sun sank over the sound, streaking the sky with apricot, purple and scarlet, the chance to get a little exercise drew several takers. She wasn't surprised when Seiji turned up the heat a notch, holding out his hands.

As before, dancing with him was so sensual that she felt they were performing some secret, amorous ritual in front of the other guests and their hosts. Instead of holding her right hand in his left in the traditional fashion, he'd placed both hands provocatively at her waist. His mouth was inches from hers.

Unable to cope with the stress of having her senses bombarded that way, Nora declined when he suggested she remain downstairs and go for a walk with him on the path overlooking the ocean when everyone else— sunburned and windblown—began heading for the house and a good night's sleep.

Though she was sorely tempted, and viewed the invitation as a chance for them to have their talk, she was a little afraid of being alone with him in such an isolated spot. Or perhaps she didn't trust herself.

"Sounds nice," she answered. "But I think I'd better get my beauty sleep. I'm pretty worn out from all the fresh air and the excitement of landing the bluefin.''

He didn't press the point. Politely accompanying her upstairs, he deposited a light good-night kiss on her cheek.

Unfortunately, though Nora really was exhausted, slumber stubbornly evaded her. When she finally managed to drift off, it was only for a short time. To her chagrin, she awoke to the realization that she'd already begun to dream of Seiji.

For once, her usual ploy of counting backward slowly from one hundred didn't have the desired effect. The disturbing thought that Seiji was in the next room, probably sleeping in the altogether, refused to be extinguished.

Desperate to get some Z's so she'd be in top form when she talked to him about Braet & Company's future in the morning, she cast about for some means of easing her tension. Exercise usually did that for her. Though the night air was chilly, the McEwen's pool, which was situated a short distance from the house, was heated. One of the other guests had mentioned it in passing earlier that evening.

She decided a solitary swim under the stars would be the perfect thing to relax her, help her get the rest she needed. Putting on the two-piece suit she'd brought, which had been designed in a retro, 1950's style, and covering it for warmth with the thick terry robe their hosts had provided, she stepped out into the hall. None of the doors had any light leaking from under them. Her footsteps soundless in the terry scuffs that matched the robe, she started down the stairs.

Meanwhile, faced with a similar buildup of tension, Seiji had gone back downstairs after wishing her good-night. Fully dressed, he'd been seated in a chair hidden by the terrace's shadows for the past forty-five minutes, willing her to come to him.

Finally, about the time she'd gotten out of bed and put on her suit, he'd given up, stripped off his clothes and quietly entered the pool. He could hardly believe his eyes when Nora appeared on the path from the house, unfastened her robe and laid it across one of the chaise lounges.

She might not forgive him if he didn't make his presence known. He called to her softly. "C'mon in. Maybe I should warn you...I'm not wearing anything."

Abruptly there was nothing that appealed to her more. She glanced at the house. Without exception, the windows were dark. "All right," she conceded after a moment, "if you promise to keep your distance."

Guaranteed he'd keep to his own area of the pool, she descended the steps at the shallow end and visually located his head and shoulders so she could stay away from him.

The experience of swimming in the same pool with Seiji while the surf crashed rhythmically in the background and the same water that touched her skin lapped over his naked body stimulated her imagination to a fever pitch. Finally she'd had all the titillation she could take.

"I think I'll get out now," she announced in an unsteady voice.

To her chagrin, he followed her, not bound by any promise to behave himself on the pool apron. Accordingly she got a silvery moonlit look at his stunning physique—his broad shoulders, the well-defined muscles of his torso, the generous male attributes he made no attempt to cover.

"Seiji, I..." she began, letting the words trail off uncertainly as he settled her robe around her shoulders, affording her just enough coverage to ward off a chill.

Seconds later, his hands were beneath it, unfastening her swimsuit top and letting it fall to the pavement. "You have such a beautiful body," he whispered between kisses, caressing her nipples lightly with his fingertips as his erection pressed against her.

Half dizzy at the sensations that washed over her, penetrating to her deepest places, Nora realized that she had to stop him. And herself. If she didn't, her virginity would be forfeit.

"We have to talk," she insisted, pulling back a little.

"Now?" he asked incredulously. "I'll agree on one condition...that we do it with my tongue in your mouth."

With an uncontrollable shudder of arousal, she submitted and they were quickly kissing with almost desperate hunger. The intensity of feeling that washed over them was like that of being carried out to sea in an undertow, or buried by an avalanche.

Somehow in their hunger, they managed to bump into one of the lawn chairs, causing it to scrape against the concrete. A light went on upstairs. Before long, someone would be peering out the window.

He wasn't *wearing* anything! Gossip about their escapade would spread like wildfire. Her face on fire with embarrassment, Nora wrenched free. Unable to locate her swimsuit top, she abandoned it and ran for the house, praying she wouldn't meet anyone on the way to her room.

Chapter Four

The following morning, she sent word via the maid who appeared to make her bed and draw her bath that she had a headache and wouldn't be going downstairs for breakfast. In fact, if her hosts wouldn't consider it an affront, she hoped everyone would go sailing without her.

"Please make my apologies," she said. "Tell them I'm worn-out from a busy week. I'll look forward to seeing them at dinnertime."

The water was running full tilt in her shower when, as expected, Seiji knocked at her door. She didn't answer and after a while he went away. Waiting until she was sure everyone, including him, had left the house, she started downstairs with the intention of borrowing a bike and pedaling to Vineyard Haven. She could get some exercise. Have a late breakfast there. Figure out when and how to talk to Seiji. And do a little sightseeing without the constant pressure of having him at her elbow.

Putting on her white duck trousers and a pink cotton twinset, she cautiously headed down the stairs. She was removing one of the bikes from the rack near the estate's six-car garage and availing herself of a lock for it when she jumped at Seiji's voice beside her ear.

"Mind if I tag along?" he asked, the little parentheses beside his mouth deepening at her startled expression.

Learning that she was on her way to Vineyard Haven, he offered to go along and buy her an ice-cream cone. "We can have that talk you wanted," he suggested.

A tandem bike was available. Incredibly, given the circumstances under which they'd parted the night before, Nora found herself pedaling behind him in an inverted rendition of their limousine trip from the ferry docks the day before. At his suggestion, they secured the bike to a lamppost near an ice-cream parlor that offered a glimpse of the harbor. The unseasonably warm weather allowed them to choose an outdoor table.

"What'll it be?" Seiji asked.

A few minutes later, he was back with two medium cones—one with double-chocolate ice cream for himself, and a pineapple-coconut sherbet for Nora. Licking the drips that had already started running down her cone without actually taking a bite of it, she gazed at him and wondered how to start. Her memory of the way he'd partially undressed her and kissed her like a house afire the night before wasn't making things any easier.

"You've already guessed that I want to talk to you about the takeover attempt you're planning with regard to Braet & Company," she said at last. "But you may not understand the reason. It isn't because of any personal financial interest I might have, though I do own a few shares of stock. On the contrary, my worries are focused on my aunt Maggie, the company's chief executive officer.

"She's a wonderful person…one who's been like a mother to me and my sisters since our mom, her sister-in-law, died in a car accident ten years ago.

"The fact is, you'd probably like her. Unfortunately she's had a terrible run of luck over the past couple of years. A second divorce. Problems with the company. And now, cancer. The outcome of her treatment's anything but certain. I'm horribly afraid that, if you take over the company, she won't have anything left to live for…that she'll just give up and let the cancer take her."

In Seiji's opinion, the quiver in Nora's voice as she explained her aunt's predicament was genuine. Though she struggled not to let it, a huge tear rolled down her cheek.

He hadn't risen to the position of prominence he enjoyed in the business world by granting pleas for mercy. Hardening his heart, an organ some of his victims had expressed doubt he possessed, he listened with rising satisfaction. He had Nora exactly where he wanted her.

He gazed at her with narrowed eyes. "I'm sorry about your aunt's troubles," he said. "However, I'm sure you'll understand when I say that I can't take such considerations into account. The acquisition of Braet & Company by my conglomerate has already been set in motion."

She blinked back more tears. Trying to reach him was like beating her head against a wall. Or jamming it into a vise. "Please...don't say that," she begged. "The company's her whole life, her *child,* in a way, since she never had any children of her own. Without it to nurture, she won't have a sense of purpose."

His little shrug was marked by indifference. "It's nothing against you personally," he said in a negligent tone. "We've only just met, after all. Besides, thanks to the takeover, the value of the stock you own will skyrocket. You can sell it and make a killing, if you wish."

At Aunt Maggie's expense, Nora raged silently, anger rising in her like a flood. Aware she could blow their whole discussion if she gave in to it, she did her best to keep it under control.

"I'd never do that in a million years," she answered in the gentlest tone she could muster. "I'd gladly *give* it to her if it would make any difference. She has my proxy anyway. I'm absolutely convinced that, if the company is absorbed, she'll be dead in a couple of months. Whereas, for you, there are lots of other investments..."

The contents of his cone were melting and he pitched it into a nearby trash can. Sitting back down, he regarded her without speaking for a moment.

"To be honest, I don't see why I should feel sympathy for anyone in your family," he said at last. "The way the Braets ostracized my grandfather and grandmother, and subsequently my mother, is nothing short of scandalous."

Tempted to agree with him, at least in part, though she'd heard stories, too, about how emotionally wounded her great-grandmother had been by Jerrold's infidelity, Nora couldn't bring herself to apologize. If she did, she felt certain, he'd fling whatever amends she tried to make back into her face.

"Maggie never personally did anything to hurt you or your mother, let alone your grandmother," she reminded him. "The rift between our families was established long before she came of age. Her worst sin...and mine, I suppose...has been to let sleeping dogs lie, make no attempt to heal the breach."

Familiar with American idiom, Seiji didn't take offense. There was a certain amount of truth in what she said and he pondered it for a moment.

Sensing a glimmer of light despite his refusal, Nora decided to give him a little push. "If there's any way I can persuade you...anything you want me to do, like getting my family to apologize..." she added, framing the words like a question.

From what Seiji had heard about her father and most of her other relatives, he didn't doubt that, deep down, they were ready to sacrifice Braet & Company, not to mention Maggie's Braet's life, if either stood in the way of a takeover that would net them unearned riches. Though their pride would be hurt by what he was planning, he'd probably be doing them a favor.

Nora, on the other hand, seemed genuinely to care for her aunt, put the older woman's interests first.

"You could go to bed with me," he suggested abruptly, aware that the insulting proposal could drive her away for good. A moment later, he amended it as he realized one night of making love with her wouldn't be enough. "Be my lover," he urged, "until we tire of each other."

The color drained from Nora's face. She could scarcely believe her ears. In essence, he was asking her to be his *geisha*, his mistress—temporarily, as a way of humiliating people she loved. Though he might desire her, there wasn't any possibility of love taking root in his heart. His tough-guy attitude and thirst for vengeance didn't leave any room for it.

"I could never accept an offer like that," she told him.

Quick to take offense, Seiji lashed back. "What's the matter?" he asked cuttingly. "Do you find my Japanese ancestry that distasteful?"

By now, her tears were flowing in earnest. "On the contrary," she confessed. "I find you very attractive. Exotic. Powerful. And very sexy. It's just that I..."

Partially appeased, he waited.

"...don't sleep around," she finished. "I know. My younger sister doesn't believe it, either. But I've been saving myself for marriage with someone I could love and trust."

She was a virgin.

All but untouched since he'd handed it to her, Nora's sherbet melted all over the tabletop as they stared at each other in what quickly became a profound silence. Are there really women like this left in the world? Seiji asked himself. Sexy, polished, self-directed women who hold themselves that precious?

"Anybody on the horizon?" he asked, hoping against hope that she wouldn't say yes.

"Only in theory," she admitted. I could have loved you, under different circumstances, she thought. But that won't be possible now. We'll go our separate ways. One of these days, Aunt Maggie will die. I'll open another magazine and see your photograph.

They exchanged a minimum of words as they pedaled back to the house. "We can leave early...tomorrow morning before the gang is up, if you like,'' Seiji offered as they returned their bike to the rack.

"I'd appreciate that," Nora said, keenly aware of how badly she'd failed with him.

As she'd expected, dinner was extremely awkward. Given what she considered Seiji's indecent proposal, she could hardly bear to face him. And she realized the other guests noticed it. To her dismay, he couldn't seem to keep his eyes off her. It didn't make things any easier.

She had no way of knowing that he was wrestling with a sense of missed opportunity and failure that matched her own. She'd turned him down, as he'd known she would. The result was that he wanted her more—so much that it was like an ache consuming him.

It was only when they were seated in the back of his limousine the following morning, headed back to New York from the ferry dock at Woods Hole in a silence that had long since reached the point of being unbearable, that he knocked her socks off with a completely different proposal.

"If you're serious about saving Braet & Company for your aunt, I have an alternate plan to suggest," he said, causing a wave of goose bumps to skitter down her arms. "Instead of just sleeping together, we get married. Have sex once, to make the union official. And live together for a year before divorcing. After our first encounter, any sexual contact between us would be at your discretion."

Nora stared.

"If you agree, your aunt will get to keep her company," he elaborated softly. "The stock I own in

Braet's will be yours as part of our divorce settlement once my terms have been fulfilled. Naturally there'll be no other alimony, rehabilitative or otherwise.''

In all likelihood, if she did as he was suggesting, it would mean giving up her career as a model. The moguls who ran the New York fashion industry were quick to forget a face. Still, it would be a small price to pay if it could improve her aunt's chances of beating her illness.

Thanks to Nora's success in what was a lucrative but very tough field, she had a tidy sum of money put away in the bank, as well as a growing investment in the stock market. At the age of twenty-five, she was well poised to make a fresh start, if need be. The question was, could she make herself *do* what he was suggesting? Make love to him knowing raw desire, not tender feelings had prompted it? That revenge was all he cared about?

When she didn't reply, a wry smile twisted Seiji's mouth. ''I'll be honest with you,'' he said. ''I don't consider my position on this issue even slightly altruistic. It hasn't escaped my notice that our marriage would rattle a few cages in the Pacific Northwest.''

He doesn't have any special feelings for me, Nora thought, despite the way he can make a fire blaze inside me with the slightest touch. It's just revenge with him. A power struggle. I'd be a trophy. A tool. A means of causing humiliation.

His next words only confirmed her supposition of a moment before. ''Naturally you'd have to put your modeling career on hold and close up your New York apartment,'' he advised, ''as we'd be living in my Kyoto house, with my mother. You'd be expected to serve as a good Japanese wife despite the limits that would be placed on our sex life. That would mean making my tea and packing my box lunches. Scrubbing my back. Sleeping with me in my bed whenever I want you there.''

Nora felt as if she'd just been punched in the stomach. "I don't understand," she faltered.

"You can sleep with a person and not have sex with them. Let me repeat my terms. Sex once, at a time of my choosing, and a year of marriage. At the end of that time, I'd have my satisfaction. My stock in Braet & Company would be yours. I'll be leaving New York for Vancouver tomorrow, around 11:00 a.m. Let me know what you decide.''

He'd given her less than twenty-four hours. In an attempt to keep her cool while she considered his offer, Nora looked away and pulled out her mother-of-pearl compact to check her makeup. To her consternation, she dropped it and—his manners smooth, as usual—he bent over to retrieve it. He didn't run his hand up her leg this time, the way he had in the little cabaret after their first meal together. Still, their brief contact when he returned it was electric. She could feel its suggestiveness deep in the privacy between her legs.

He dropped her at her apartment building around noon and waited in the limousine while his driver carried her luggage upstairs. Racing to the window after the man had left, she peered through the blinds to see if Seiji would glance up. He didn't. As she watched, the driver got behind the wheel. The limousine slid smoothly into traffic and turned the corner, disappearing from view.

It had been the most unbelievable weekend she'd ever experienced. Turning away from her view of the street, she wondered where it had left them.

She had a strong feeling that, if she refused Seiji's offer or simply let the time he'd given her run out, she wouldn't see him again. I could use a drink, she thought, heading for the kitchen and fixing herself an unaccustomed Scotch on the rocks. Seconds later, she was pouring it into the sink. I need a clear head to think this through, she realized, staring at the cluster of leftover ice cubes. The buzz of liquor won't help.

Brewing herself a cup of herbal tea with honey instead, and changing into a pair of sweats that had seen better days, she started to pace the confines of her apartment. Usually hanging around home in old clothes on a Sunday afternoon was something of a treat, though she seldom had anyone she considered special to read the paper with. Today, the place felt flat, amazingly empty without Seiji in it. She only hoped she hadn't fallen for him.

It wasn't likely on such short acquaintance. Or at least that was what she tried to tell herself. Instead of worrying about such things, she needed to confront and analyze the decision she faced. Did she have the guts to give up everything and live with him in Japan for a year? Spending that much time under his roof, in the constant company of an older woman who probably despised her because she was one of Jerrold's American descendants, would be extremely difficult.

I'll have to do it, she decided finally, leaving off pacing and hugging her arms. Give Seiji what he wants and let his mother's dislike wash off me like rain. At least the deed will take place within the bounds of wedlock.

She guessed that to some, she'd be compromising her principles. But she didn't regard it that way. The fact is, I'm honouring them. Helping Aunt Maggie hang on to her reason for living is far more important than denying Seiji Amundsen his long sought vengeance. The essence of me will remain untouched.

Her family would be horrified, of course. Too easily, she could imagine her father, Stephen Braet, raving to his current wife, Alison, that his daughter was a traitor for even *associating* with Seiji Amundsen. But then he hadn't been to see his ailing sister once while she'd been in the hospital. His opinion didn't count for much.

Lawrence Braet, her obese, hypochondriac grandfather, and Elwin Braet, Jr., her caustic, sniveling second cousin, would cut her to shreds with their malicious gossip. Her great-aunt Enid, a terminally proper maiden lady, would behave as if she'd fallen off the face of the earth into the fires of eternal damnation.

Placed in such an awkward, emotionally difficult position, Nora would make it a point to take care of herself. Whatever happened during the year she and Seiji spent together, she wouldn't let herself fall in love with him. Perceptive enough to figure it out immediately if she stumbled into that mode, he'd take advantage. The humiliation would be just too much.

Picking up the phone and curling up on her living-room couch as if it were a favorite lap, she dialed Darien's number. For once, she didn't get the answering machine. Her sister was at home instead of sprinting from one trauma victim to another in the emergency room.

"Hi, Dare. How's Aunt Maggie doing?" she asked.

It seemed Darien had stopped by their aunt's room shortly before leaving the hospital an hour earlier. "Hard to say," she reported. "Probably about the same. What's the latest on your end?"

Nora hesitated. "Promise you won't tell Steph, that you'll let me break the news to her in my own way?"

"Break *what* news?" Plainly Darien had caught the shaky note in her voice.

"I've come to a meeting of the minds with Seiji Amundsen. He's agreed to sign over his Braet's stock to me. I'll receive clear title to it a year from now, if all goes as planned. In the meantime, the company will be out of danger."

"Thank God! Maggie'll be so relieved..." Darien's gut-level response trailed off as if she were digesting the details of Nora's statement, including some she hadn't articulated. "Why a year?" she demanded. "With Amundsen, there has to be a quid pro quo."

By telling Darien, Nora was already taking the plunge. "He wanted me to be his mistress in exchange for any concessions he might make," she admitted. "You know how I feel about that sort of thing. I turned him down flat. He counteroffered marriage." Her voice a little breathless, she set forth his terms.

Darien was audibly distressed. "You can't do what he's suggesting!" she exclaimed.

"The alternative is letting Maggie lose hope," Nora replied stubbornly. "Or having sex with him on a regular basis without benefit of a wedding ring until he gets tired of me. Either way, my career and my self-respect will suffer. I should consider myself lucky he's willing to keep me an honest woman, I guess."

Waiting until the last possible moment, as if somehow that would make things easier, Nora called Seiji at his hotel the following morning. Having given up hope of hearing from her, he was packing freshly laun-

dered shirts in an expensive leather valise preparatory
to departing for the airport when the phone rang.

"Yes?" he responded impatiently.

"It's Nora," she said, the simple acknowledgment
of her identity sticking in her throat.

Was it *possible?* He shored up his defenses. She
might not be calling to accept his offer. "What can I
do for you?" he asked.

A fierce little silence rested between them. "I, um,
have decided to say yes to your proposal," she whispered.

He was both elated and confounded. He hadn't realized how much he'd wanted to prevail. *"Mo ichido
yutay kudasai?"* he asked, the intensity of his voice
escalating a notch. Seconds later, he realized he'd spoken in Japanese. He repeated the question in English.
"Say that again, please? I can't quite believe my ears."

Her reply was a little clipped. "You weren't mistaken. I accept your offer of marriage. If I want my
aunt to make it, I don't have any other choice."

Suddenly cognizant of the bitter irony he'd created
by shackling their strong, natural attraction to a marriage of convenience, he asked if she could meet him
in Vancouver at the end of the week. "I own a condominium overlooking the harbor there," he said. "If
it won't put you in too much of a bind, we'll continue
on to Japan next Sunday evening."

Aware he expected her to say something, Nora murmured that she probably could keep to that schedule.

She sounded like a zombie. Incredibly distant. Well,
who could blame her? He tried to imagine how it
would feel, to be thrust into her shoes. Though it
aroused his empathy, the exercise didn't prompt him
to let her off the hook.

"I'll have my lawyer draw up a prenuptial agreement and your lawyer can go over it by fax," he added in a cool, businesslike tone. "If there are any small points of disagreement, I'm sure we can work them out."

Canceling all her upcoming modeling assignments to the distress of her agent and subletting her apartment for the duration, Nora put her artwork, books and personal effects in storage and packed as well as she could for a year spent halfway around the world. She left New York early on Thursday morning, in order to spend a little time with Maggie in Seattle before leaving the country.

A wizard with coordinates, who knew how to pack light, Nora toted just two carry-on bags on the flight west. The bulk of her wardrobe had been packed into several large cartons and stashed in the hold of the 747. Instead of arranging to pick them up in Washington state and go through the whole thing again when she boarded their flight to Japan from Vancouver, she'd checked them through to Kansai International Airport, which served Kyoto in addition to the bustling cities of Osaka and Kobe. One of Seiji's servants had been instructed to collect them there.

Several people eyed her on the flight, no doubt recognizing her from some ad or magazine cover. But no one spoke to her. It was as if she were traveling in a vacuum, suspended between the life she knew and the one she hadn't tasted yet.

She still found it difficult to believe what was happening. Seiji must really hate the Braets if he's willing to go to such lengths to hurt and embarrass us, she thought, gazing out at the sere Montana landscape. Sophisticated as she was, thanks to the time she'd spent in New York, her mind shied away from what it would be like to let him make love to her. Yet she kept returning to it, as if she hoped to find, beneath his passion and arrogance, more heartfelt possibilities.

Her aunt was sitting up in bed when she arrived at the hospital, after dropping off her bags via cab at Maggie's Lake Union apartment. Though Maggie was still weak and seemed to have lost more weight, she claimed to be feeling a little better.

"Looks like I might pull through...this time," she said with an ironic twist to her mouth after they'd embraced and kissed. "My doctor seems to think so. Aren't those roses beautiful?" She gestured toward her tray table. "Darien brought them. She's been an angel."

Nora smiled and nodded. She was doing the right thing. That fact was abundantly clear, now that she was standing in Maggie's hospital room.

"I have a present for you, too...one that ought to help get you up and out of here," she said, opening the blind so Maggie could see out the window. "At the moment, it's invisible, so I didn't bother to wrap it."

Maggie's lips parted in a gesture of delight and anticipation Nora had unconsciously borrowed for many a photo session. "What is it?" she asked with childlike eagerness.

"Actually I managed to get an option on a huge block of Braet & Company stock. I'll be able to acquire it at a very favorable price. With what the family owns, it should make Braet & Company takeover-proof."

Her aunt gaped. "Darling! Are you *serious?*"

Nora's million-dollar smile was at full wattage for

the first time since Seiji had made his startling proposal. "You can relax and get better. The company will be there for you when you're ready to go back to work."

Holding out her arms, Maggie enveloped her in a bear hug. "Sweet child," she murmured, shaking her head. "Your father doesn't deserve you. *I* don't."

In the next breath, she was demanding to know the full story of how Nora had pulled off such a coup.

"It involves a man," Nora admitted.

Maggie's eyes sparkled with delight.

Aware she'd have to tell her aunt at least part of the truth, Nora offered to spill "the details" in a moment. "First I have some news," she revealed. "I'm going to be working in Japan for a while."

An expression of distress fled across Maggie's features and was quickly extinguished. She moved over and patted the edge of the bed. "Time for a woman-to-woman gab session," she declared.

Though Nora was forced to disclose her new man's identity, in part because Maggie would almost certainly find out about it anyway, she didn't breathe a word about the finer points of their arrangement. Instead she allowed her aunt to think she and Seiji had fallen hard for each other when she'd approached him about the takeover.

With something of her customary spark, Maggie indulged in a smile or two over her brother's too predictable reaction. "If I were you, I wouldn't tell him anything about your plans until after you've left the country," she advised.

Nora rolled her eyes. "I don't plan to."

To her surprise, Maggie didn't disparage the connection. Instead she commented it was long past time that the estranged branches of the Braet family be reintegrated. "It's the kind of thing you think about now and then as the years pass, but fail to do anything about," she acknowledged ruefully. "One of life's little undone tasks that weigh down your spirit and come back to haunt you."

Nora visited her aunt again that evening and twice again the following day. Their parting on Thursday evening was characterized by hugs and smiles that had to fight their way through tears. Without making a direct reference to her illness and the odds that it might prove fatal, Maggie urged Nora not to stay away too long.

"Try to get back by Christmas if you can," she entreated. "Bring Mr. Amundsen. That should spice up the annual family celebration!"

During her brief stopover in Seattle, Nora also joined Darien for a meal in their favorite Thai restaurant and phoned Stephanie at her cabin near Snoqualmie. After swearing her younger sister to secrecy, she unveiled the truth about her plans.

Stephanie was shocked enough to forgo any remarks about Nora having taken her suggestions too seriously.

"I'm trusting you to keep this information absolutely secret," Nora emphasized. "I've told Maggie as much as she can safely absorb in her condition. I don't want her to know the details."

On Saturday, Nora postponed her reunion with Seiji as long as possible. Instead of flying directly to Vancouver, she took the ferry from Seattle to Victoria, connecting with another ferry to the British Columbian capital city from Swartz Bay at the last possible moment. Though she tried to stay calm, meditating breeze-blown by the rail on the latter leg of her journey as they chugged past thickly forested islands over brightly hammered water, a knot of troubled anticipation formed in her chest.

Would she be able to endure the coming year of self-sacrifice she'd described to Maggie as a serendipitous blend of business and romance? Or wouldn't she? Her instinctive physical and emotional attraction to Seiji had upset her deeply. If she gave free rein to it, she realized, she'd find herself in a profoundly heart-wrenching situation.

Chapter Five

A uniformed man with a cardboard sign proclaiming her name in handprinted capital letters met her at the ferry dock south of the city, in Tsawwassen. He bowed deeply when she approached. "Miss Braet?" he asked in his heavy Japanese accent.

It was all she could do to keep from bowing in return. "That's me," she responded with her Western informality.

"I take your luggage, please."

They quickly left the dock area in a limousine that contained a forgotten pair of men's sunglasses and several business magazines printed in Japanese—evidence that Seiji had used it recently.

As he'd told her, the building where he had his Vancouver condominium was situated near the downtown, overlooking the harbor and the Royal Rowing Club. Parking in the underground garage, the chauffeur whisked Nora and her luggage to the top floor in a sleekly efficient, chrome-and-mahogany elevator.

A few seconds later, the chauffeur was inserting a magnetized card into the appropriate slot and opening the door. Though her peripheral vision took in the condo's simple but sumptuous living area with its plush, off-white contemporary couches, gleaming *tansu* chests and intricately patterned, wall-hung collection of antique kimonos, her gaze sped straight to Seiji the way iron filings race to a magnet.

He was standing with his back to them, a barefoot, solitary figure in slacks and a sweater staring out a bank of sliding glass balcony doors that overlooked the water. Though the door had opened without a sound and their footsteps sank noiselessly into the thick, neutral-colored carpet, he seemed instantly aware of their presence. He turned. Stormy and difficult to read, the way Nora remembered them, his eyes met hers. She almost gasped at the uncertainty, the hunger, the sense of incipient *ownership* that was mirrored there.

Seconds later, he'd crossed the space that separated them and greeted her with a blunt, openmouthed, wholly proprietary kiss, his hands imprisoning her upper arms as his chauffeur bowed and disappeared from view with her bags.

Loosening his grip, he drew her more fully into his embrace. Ah, but she's warm and delicious to hold with the bloom of cool air on her cheeks, he thought, gathering her close. So beautiful and spirited. I want her so much it's like an ache in my flesh. Though he couldn't afford to let her into his heart, everything in him longed to hurtle forward in time to the moment when, physically, at least, they'd become one person.

Despite her vow to remain unaffected by any advances he might make, a stab of arousal pierced Nora to the quick as he inserted his tongue into her mouth.

What wouldn't he ask of her? she wondered. That she learn to care for him, when it would almost certainly be a one-way street? Plead with him to ravish her again and again, in mindless repudiation of the bargain they'd struck?

Already she was putty in his hands, a fragile ship of naiveté adrift on a tide of helplessness. Pressed against her lower body, the hot, hard evidence of his arousal was causing her sanity to disintegrate.

Outside, dusk was gathering like the folds of a velvet robe. Abruptly he let her go. She almost stumbled. Lightly supporting her, he gave her one of his more enigmatic smiles. It was as if the sudden, passionate interlude between them had been a figment of her imagination—never taken place.

"You must be tired after your journey," he commented, his rough baritone solicitous. "Come have a drink with me on the balcony. We can eat outdoors this evening, if you like. As you may already know, there'll be a full moon tonight. Fireworks have been planned in honor of a visit by British royalty."

Slipping off her shoes in deference to what was probably a Japanese household custom, Nora allowed him to lead her out past the sliding-glass doors. His view of the harbor was spectacular—a panorama that included the rising moon, scores of small boats taking up their positions for the show, lights winking on in the frieze of skyscrapers that lined the river's bank. Reflections fled jewel-toned into the water.

Conversation was difficult. It advanced in fits and starts as they dined on Japanese beer and *teppanyaki* prepared over a charcoal grill by the same manservant who had brought Nora from the ferry dock. She ate the deliciously charred meat and the spicy if somewhat plain lettuce salad that accompanied it with wooden chopsticks, as Seiji did, acquitting herself honorably with them.

Overhead, the moon seemed to grow heavier, becoming an increasingly overripe orb as the evening progressed. After his manservant removed their plates and brought out a small selection of sweets, their conversation backslid almost to the point of silence as each tried to imagine how the bargain they'd struck would work out. Or so Nora conjectured. She couldn't actually read Seiji's mind, though she gave it her best shot. As a result, she almost jumped when he shattered their lengthy reverie to murmur that formal moon viewing was a popular pastime in Japan.

"You mentioned your first experience on our trip to Martha's Vineyard," she reminded him.

"So I did." A little smile apologized for his forgetfulness. "I'll take you to my country place sometime...the one where I keep my falcons," he offered. "Maybe even invite some friends to join us. The viewing from there is spectacular."

A few minutes later, the fireworks got under way, causing cheers and applause to go up from boaters and people gathered along the sea walls. Time seemed to slow its forward progress as the sky was illuminated by starbursts, pinwheels, disintegrating fountains of red and green light, rapidly blossoming chrysanthemums.

At last the panorama was over. Boaters hauled anchor. Viewing parties began to break up.

"Maybe it's time for *us* to say good-night," Seiji suggested softly, getting to his feet and extending a hand to her. "We'd do well to get a good night's sleep."

"You're probably right," she acknowledged.

In response, he led her to the door of the guest room she'd occupy and gave her a little bow, as if to promise he wouldn't rush things beyond the speed she could tolerate.

"Morning will come soon enough," he added. "And we have a big ocean to cross. A case of jet lag will be waiting for us."

Despite the deep comfort of the Western-style bed she occupied, Nora spent a restless night. It was nearly 4:00 a.m. when finally she sank into a profound, more refreshing slumber. As a result, she didn't awaken until shortly before 9:00 a.m.

Half tempted to pad in robe and pajamas to the kitchen and partake of a reviving cup of tea or coffee, she forced herself to shower, dress in the relaxed outfit she'd wear for the flight and put on her makeup. To an extent she was just beginning to realize, her relationship with Seiji would be a board game of strategy and sensuality, a test of will and determination. She didn't want to play without putting on her war paint.

Accordingly it was something of a letdown when she emerged from her room to find the manservant finishing the last-minute packing and Seiji hard at work in his office, using both fax machine and phone as he issued orders to various underlings around the globe. A glimpse of him in navy blue sweats was visible through a partly open doorway.

By now it was almost nine-thirty.

"Good morning, Miss Braet," the manservant greeted her. "Mr. Amundsen can't be disturbed right now. You like I fix you breakfast? We go to the airport in an hour."

Before long, the die would be cast. Remembering

her boast to Aunt Maggie that she'd taken care of Braet & Company's problems, Nora accepted orange juice, coffee and toast, spent twenty minutes on a second telephone line, promising her aunt that she'd keep in touch.

She was ready in low-heeled shoes, tobacco brown wool slacks, a silver-gray silk blouse and mohair tweed jacket, with knitted slippers, a sleep mask and an inflatable neck pillow stashed in her carry-on bag by the time Seiji emerged in suit and tie, ready to depart.

"All set?" he asked, the words resonating with a meaning that went beyond their journey to the airport.

Nora nodded. I wouldn't have come this far if I didn't plan to carry out my part of our agreement, she thought with silent resolve.

Thanks to their first-class tickets, they were able to sweep past the long lines of coach passengers that filled the terminal. Clearing customs and baggage control with its explosives-sniffing dogs took a little longer. By the time they made it to the gate, the agent was already calling them for boarding.

Insofar as the rest of the world knows, we're a couple though we've just met and barely know each other, Nora reflected as Seiji handed over their tickets for inspection. The leather-upholstered seats they'd been assigned were wide and comfortable. Smiling and speaking briefly in Japanese to Seiji, a flight attendant helped stow their carry-on luggage in an overhead compartment.

Boarding the rest of the plane took roughly half an hour. We'll be on our way at any moment, Nora thought as they edged back from the gate. Unless I can convince Seiji to let me visit Seattle now and then, it'll be a year until I see Aunt Maggie. And I'm afraid to leave her for that long.

Slowly they taxied to the outbound runway. At a signal from the tower, the pilot increased their ground speed, demanding the maximum output from his 747's jet engines. Seconds later, they were lifting off, climbing at a sharp angle to the ground and banking steeply above the channel her ferry to Tsawwassen had plied. Vancouver Island stretched out beneath them. As Nora watched, they emerged over the iridescent shimmer of the Pacific Ocean. All my moorings have been cut, she thought, a lump forming in her throat. I'm adrift between two lives, two continents.

Seiji appeared not to notice the emotional distance she'd put between them by the time they'd reached their cruising altitude. In her shoes, he supposed, he'd be experiencing a similar tumult of emotions. Instead of making an effort to converse with her, he accepted a small glass of sake from the flight attendant, settled back with stereo earphones plugged into his ears and pulled some business reports from his briefcase.

Turning down an offer of alcohol but accepting a Perrier, Nora was grateful to be left to her own devices. She stared out at the panorama of clouds and water, then leafed negligently through a Kyoto guidebook, as if she were a tourist preparing for an extended vacation instead of a bride-to-be, anticipating a year of marriage to a man she yearned for physically but couldn't allow herself to love.

Later, she rummaged in her carry-on bag and withdrew an English translation of the classic Japanese novel, *The Tale of Gengi*, which she'd purchased on a whim at a Seattle bookstore.

Written by a woman in the eleventh century, the novel had always been one of Seiji's favorites. "It's better in the original," he informed Nora softly, his arm brushing hers as he unplugged his earphones for a moment.

I don't want his touch to arouse me the way it does, Nora thought. Or to drink the scent of his aftershave too deeply into my nostrils. Though I could have cared for him under different circumstances, thanks to the deal we made, I'll never do anything of the sort.

"As you're probably aware, I don't speak a word of Japanese," she reminded him somewhat distantly. "I don't have a prayer of learning to read the ideographs that serve as your alphabet. This is the best I can do, I'm afraid."

Some time later, after dinner had been served and cleared, and an American movie with Japanese subtitles had been screened, the cabin was darkened to allow the passengers to get some rest on something approximating their usual schedules. To avoid conversation, Nora pretended to drift into slumber almost immediately. She wasn't aware of the point when dissembling became the real thing.

Watching as she slept, Seiji remarked to himself that the confident, self-directed model he was engaged to marry, who had the New York fashion world at her feet, looked as defenseless as a thirteen-year-old. I want to know everything she's thinking, everything she feels, he realized. The subject of her dreams at this very moment.

Despite his sleeping around, the many women who'd come and gone in his life, he'd never experienced anything like the way he and Nora struck sparks from each other. It occurred to him for the first time that maybe he should have pledged to leave Braet & Company to its own devices until Maggie Braet was out of the picture. If he had, asking nothing in return, he might have been able to court Nora in the usual manner. Unhappily, thanks to his pride and strong sense of rejection by his grandfather's American family, that opportunity was no longer available to him.

Because of Seiji's VIP status and the considerable stock he owned in the carrier he'd chosen for their flight, their arrival at Kansai and progress through customs were facilitated by an airline employee. Yet another limousine driver met them at the curb. They were quickly on their way to Kyoto, which was some miles distant, via a six-lane expressway from Airport Island to the mainland at Rinku Machi.

Never having visited Japan before, Nora craned her neck to stare at the immense Kobe-Osaka shipyards, the distant mountains, a jumble of advertising billboards, "parlors" for playing *pachinko,* which Seiji explained was a vertical version of pinball that attracted gamblers. A seemingly endless parade of smallish houses, roofed in tile or tin, flashed by, overhung by electrical wires and guarded by utility poles. Each had its own neatly tended vegetable garden, spread out like a pocket handkerchief.

When they reached the outskirts of Kyoto, Seiji ordered their driver to "go through the city." He used his cellular phone to warn his mother of their impending arrival. According to what he'd told Nora on the plane, he'd broken the news of their plan to marry by phone to her several days before their departure. Keenly aware of her lifelong grudge against her father's American descendants and, constrained by her strong sense of propriety, he'd neglected to explain their union's temporary nature. Or the fact that it was part business deal, part Faustian bargain with, for him, a gratifying emotional payoff.

The city itself, with its unimaginative modern hotels, huge concrete block of a station and ugly, needle-shaped tower stabbing the sky, was something of a disappointment for Nora, who'd always thought of it as the epitome of traditional Japanese culture. Still, glittering shops promising an array of esoteric treasures beckoned. A profusion of shrines and temples invited her to explore.

Massive, colorful, the famous Heian Shrine blocked their way and they had to turn left in order to go around it. Nora couldn't help but be drawn by the sense of power and serenity it exuded.

By the time they'd passed through the city's urban neighborhoods to wind up its greener, more heavily wooded northern slopes toward the place of all the places he owned that Seiji called home, he'd pointed out a number of interesting sights she might want to visit and mentioned others that were off their route or hidden from view.

"Kyoto isn't what it was when my mother was growing up, or so she tells me," he admitted. "But it still has many delightful, out-of-the-way places. I think you'll like it here."

To her surprise, Nora thought so, too. Maybe it won't be so bad, scrubbing his back now and then, she decided, attempting to gloss over the aspect of their bargain she feared would most compromise and embarrass her. With time, I'll be able to control my feelings for him. Meanwhile, there won't be any runways or 5:00 a.m. makeup calls, no posing half-naked in designer suits and blouses no decent woman would dream of wearing to the office. I'll get to explore the city to my heart's content.

Seiji's contemporary yet somehow traditional house, situated high in the hills above famed Kinkakuji Temple, away from the urban sprawl, was stunning in its simplicity. Its steep, blue ceramic-tile roof caught and held the sun's brilliance while its weathered, silver-gray cypress exterior hinted at shade and rest, expressing a softer note. Gaps between the pines, carefully pruned maples and bamboo that surrounded it afforded glimpses of a distant landscape, confirming that the house had been built on a promontory of sorts. The uncluttered elegance of the place sang to Nora at every level.

With a little flourish, they pulled up on a gravel turn-around beside an irregular stone path that appeared to lead along one side of the structure, beneath a roofed, wide-open gate.

"My mother has caused the ceremonial gate to be opened in honor of our arrival," Seiji said, making no move to get out of the limousine. "The smaller gate, which is closed at the moment, is dedicated to everyday use."

She didn't comment. "How shall I address her?" she asked instead, suddenly uneasy about the kind of reception she was likely to get.

"'Mrs. Amundsen' should be all right," he answered. Reaching into his trouser pocket, he took out a small velvet box. "I'd like you to have this before we go inside," he added, removing an exquisite marquise-style diamond solitaire set in platinum and slipping it onto the ring finger of her left hand. "It'll be yours to keep once the conditions of our bargain have been met."

Astonished and more than a little offended by the implication that she might attempt to keep the ring without carrying out her obligation to him, Nora was tempted to return it as he helped her out of the limo's rear seat and led her up the path, which abruptly turned a corner into a secluded entry garden. She decided not to, as it would cause an argument.

Aware of her struggle with herself over the point, he didn't let on. "This is the *kutsunugi-ishi* or 'taking-off-shoes-stone,'" he informed her, indicating a flat, artistically irregular slab of granite that was embedded in textured cement below a broad wooden step and the slightly higher entry to the house itself, which was framed by partly open, sliding wood panels. "Because this is a conventional house in the sense that the floors are covered with thick, soft *tatami* mats, we don't wear shoes indoors."

For some reason, Nora found the idea of meeting Aiko Braet Amundsen in her stocking feet somewhat daunting. She pushed the feeling aside, telling herself that her experience working before large audiences and hypercritical fashion photographers would be an enormous help.

"I'm happy to meet you, too," she answered, responding calmly in kind to her prospective mother-in-law's graceful bow and dispassionate, heavily accented greeting in English.

Short in stature and quite gray though her upswept hair retained a little of what Nora guessed had been its original dark luster, Aiko didn't smile or allow any sort of expression to cross her face. She wore a simply patterned kimono and *tabi*, the white Japanese "house socks" reminiscent of foot-mittens, with a separate segment for the big toe. Though she was Jerrold

Braet's daughter, she hadn't inherited much in the way of looks from him.

Instinct told Nora that Aiko would cooperate with Seiji's whim if forced to do so to keep the peace while undercutting her whenever she had a chance. A stray comment she'd read somewhere returned to haunt her. In Japan, it had declared, a wife was expected to care for her husband's mother—be ruled by her every wish and demand.

This isn't going to be easy, Nora thought, released a few minutes later for a much needed nap in the room she'd occupy until she and Seiji spoke their vows. Only the thought of Aunt Maggie—and, ironically, her own strong unwillingness to be separated from Seiji just yet—kept her from phoning for a taxi and heading back to the airport.

Several hours later, she, Seiji and his mother shared an evening meal of *ishikari nabe,* which was prepared in front of them by a kneeling female servant as they sat on floor cushions at a low table. The dish, which contained salmon, mushrooms, greens and squares of grilled tofu plus some other ingredients Nora didn't recognize, was stirred and simmered in a ceramic casserole filled with seaweed broth and *miso* over a gas ring that stood directly on the tabletop. To her surprise, she quite liked its taste.

The dinner conversation wasn't equally successful, with Seiji getting little help from her or his mother as he gamely introduced subject after subject. Though by now it was somewhat cool outside, the translucent *shoji* screens that covered one wall were pushed back to reveal the garden, a carefully cultivated, seemingly natural space that featured several large, irregularly shaped

rocks, a stone lantern and a lily pond fed by a bamboo
water spout. Nora took refuge in gazing at it whenever
she wasn't required to speak or pay attention.

Seiji took her outside to see it in more detail following the meal, eventually leading her down a winding
path through the trees to a stone-rimmed overlook. The
lights of Kyoto spread out before them, sparkling in
the dusk.

She thought he might kiss her. Instead, after a few
minutes, he bowed to her and announced that he was
returning to the house. Unlike her, he'd spent the re-
mainder of the afternoon attending to business matters.
With jet lag tugging at his eyelids, he was ready for a
bath and a soak.

Nora knew what that meant. Her mental picture of
him naked, being scrubbed by one of the female servants, evoked a sharp pang of arousal. But it was nothing to what she felt when Aiko approached her a few
minutes later to say Seiji and the maid were waiting
for her.

"I...don't understand," she protested with a sinking
feeling in the pit of her stomach.

"He wants you to watch...learn how to bathe a man
properly," the older woman informed her without expression.

Chapter Six

Someone had left a dark blue cotton *yukata* reverse-patterned with white chrysanthemums on Nora's futon-style bed. Thoroughly disconcerted over what Seiji was asking of her but unwilling to risk undoing their bargain by refusing him, she slipped into the lightweight garment.

Moments later, she was rapping reluctantly on the wooden frame of the sliding interior panel Aiko had indicated. From the other side, a woman's voice murmured something submissive in Japanese. Taking the words as an invitation to enter, Nora slid the panel open and stepped inside the room.

Seiji's ceramic-tile, cedar-lined bath was situated a step below the area where he slept. Beyond the deep, traditional cedar tub, which appeared big enough to accommodate several persons, the *fusuma* or sliding interior panels had been left open to reveal his large, comfortable-looking futon and a pair of partly open *shoji* that led to the garden.

Contrary to Aiko's assertion, he wasn't there yet. Wearing a pale pink bra and matching panties that resembled lightweight nylon shorts, the female servant who'd cooked their evening meal waited beside a low stool. Next to her on the floor, by a drain that had been cemented into the tiles, she'd placed a steaming wooden bucket of soapy water along with a dipper and an array of sponges and natural-fiber brushes. Several thick terry towels were piled on the tub's rim.

The object of Nora's gaze, the servant-girl shyly lowered her lashes. She's as embarrassed to have me watch as I'll be, forced to make up an unwilling audience of one, Nora realized. No doubt the latter situation is exactly what Seiji has in mind.

According to a guidebook she'd purchased in Seattle along with her copy of *Gengi,* mixed public bathing was a long-standing tradition in Japan. That being the case, she doubted if the man she'd agreed to marry would take her feelings into consideration and wear swim trunks. Still, mundane as it might be to him, he'd probably get a rush from parading naked in front of her.

Visions of how he'd looked, unclothed and dripping on the pool apron at Martha's Vineyard, returned to haunt her. Yet she knew seeing him that way wouldn't engender her most awkward moments. *Those* would come about when the maid was required to wash his private area. If he responded to her attentions, Nora would sink with humiliation—even as she imagined herself evoking that kind of reaction from him.

Seconds later, he was walking into the room and greeting them both with a casual little bow. Though he didn't smile at Nora's obvious discomfort, he couldn't keep the telltale quote marks that usually accompanied amusement with him from deepening beside his mouth as he took off his *yukata* and set it aside.

He wasn't wearing anything beneath it. Prepared for that eventuality though she was, Nora all but gasped at the sheer beauty of his tawny, well-developed body and stunning male attributes. He must realize what an extraordinary specimen he is, she thought, fighting back the waves of sensual tumult that washed over her despite her scruples. Any number of women have probably told him so.

To think that, at some point, he'd undress her. Press his naked body to hers. Enter the place where no man had gone before and plumb it to its depths. When that moment came, there wouldn't be any guest room for her to run to. Or escape of any sort. Though her cheeks radiated heat and the moist privacy between her legs confounded her by responding physically to the imagined scenes that filled her thoughts, she stubbornly refused to look away from him.

Good, thought Seiji with satisfaction, aware of her distress and reluctant stimulation—not to mention totally unfazed by his slight, corresponding tumescence. She may not want to be here, but she'll look her fill. She isn't cold. Or indifferent. The sparks we'll strike when we become lovers will melt us to red-hot ingots.

Though she couldn't know it, his partial response was due to the fact that she'd be forced to watch for a good five minutes or so while another woman ministered to him, and not to that woman's anticipated attentions. Being bathed by Michiko was pleasant, to be sure. But it wasn't much different from having her prepare a cup of tea for him.

With a little grunt that betrayed his satisfaction with the erotic tableau he'd created, he sat down on the stool, wiped his face with the steaming cloth the maid handed him and nodded that she was free to begin her task. She began by shampooing and rinsing his thick, dark hair. Next, ladling some of the hot, soapy water from her bucket over his shoulders, she scrubbed them with one of her brushes, working her way down his back with ample attention to the benefits of massage in addition to cleanliness.

Finished, she moved around to his chest. Though his eyes appeared to be shut with pleasure, Nora guessed he was actually watching her through narrowed slits. I'll be damned if I'll reward him for arranging this outrageous tableau by playing the overwhelmed, reluctantly stimulated female, she vowed. Keeping her face as free of expression as she sometimes made it when she paraded down the runway, she knelt on the tiles with the easy grace of her profession and threw her gaze out of focus.

She couldn't maintain her bored, uninterested facade when the woman's ministrations moved lower. Like the maid, who modestly averted her eyes as she performed the most intimate part of her task, she looked away. She was more relieved than she could say when the woman continued lower, to scrub Seiji's legs and feet.

Unfortunately the embarrassment he'd arranged for her wasn't over yet. She was forced to scramble back to her feet and get out of the way when the maid scooped fresh pitchers of steaming water from the tub and poured them over him, causing it and the suds that had covered him to splash far and wide before flowing down the drain.

Thoroughly clean and invigorated, Seiji got to his feet and bowed to the servant girl, eliciting a bow from her in return. With almost pathetic eagerness, she picked up her brushes and sponges and scurried from the room.

Nora didn't move.

"So," said Seiji, facing her dripping wet and naked, his muscular legs planted slightly apart. "I trust you've got the idea?"

"It looks easy enough," she snapped back with all the nonchalance she could muster despite her strong discomfort over being alone with him when he was in that state. "Rather like bathing a baby…"

"Ah, but I'm hardly an infant, in case you didn't notice."

A small silence rested between them, fraught with rebellion and unwilling shivers of arousal on Nora's part. "May I go now?" she asked after a moment.

Despite their strong physical attraction to each other, Seiji realized, she'd continue to behave like a sacrificial lamb forced to accept dishonor at his hands. So what if she did? It was what he'd bargained for, wasn't it? Why did he suddenly wish for something completely different?

"In a moment," he murmured.

Climbing into the tub, he sat down, sinking into the steaming water up to his neck with a little sigh of satisfaction. Bathing was one of his favorite pleasures. But not the ultimate one. For *that*, he needed a partner.

At the moment, there was only one partner in all the world that he wanted.

"You're free to join me, if you like," he invited lazily. "I won't tell my mother if you won't. Of course, you'll have to take off your clothes and scrub down first."

The mental picture of what it would be like to join him in the tub and let him caress her body as the bathwater rippled around them caused goose bumps to race over Nora's skin. It also galvanized her to action.

"I remember agreeing to bathe you after we're married, if that's something traditional for a wife to do," she retorted before stalking from the room. "But not to bathe *with* you. For that, you'll have to find yourself a mistress!"

Despite the embarrassing, suggestive memories of the tableau Seiji had arranged that continued to dance in her head and the unaccustomed hardness of her futon, which made her long for her bed in New York, Nora managed to drift into a sound and reviving sleep. A glance at her watch when she opened her eyes the following morning told her it was past 10:00 a.m. Kyoto time. She hardly ever awakened that late. What would Seiji and his mother think? That she was a spoiled, self-indulgent American unused to working for a living, when that was far from the case?

Calculating the corresponding time in New York or Seattle would have been an exercise in frustration and Nora didn't attempt it. Still she knew that, during the morning hours, at least, Japan was a day ahead of the U.S., thanks to its location west of the international dateline. For her, that fact translated to confusion. It was as if she'd been plucked from her everyday life in America by a giant hand and set down on a foreign planet.

I hope Seiji's left for his office by now so I won't have to face him this morning, she thought, showering in the cramped Western-style bath that adjoined her room. After drying off, she dressed in a pair of loose-fitting slacks and a cotton sweater. When she put in an appearance in the *zashiki,* which roughly translated to a living room, she found Aiko seated on a floor cushion at a small portable desk, making what appeared to be some sort of list in Japanese characters.

"You're up late," the older woman said with a frown in her perfect yet utterly foreign-sounding English, her dark eyes holding a measure of criticism. "The servants can't stop their work to make breakfast for you at this hour. I'll order *sencha*..."

At her summons, a cup of steaming green tea was quickly produced.

"Where's Seiji?" Nora asked casually, after taking a sip. "At his office, I suppose."

Aiko gave her a pitying look. "Didn't he tell you? He's gone to Singapore on business. He won't return until the end of the week."

Going away without saying goodbye is his way of letting me know he has no tender feelings for me, not to mention forcing me to sink or swim in my new environment, Nora thought. He's also made it plain to his mother that I don't count for much. Well, I can do without him. There's nothing enjoyable about being forced to watch a performance like the one he put on last night for my benefit.

In the same breath, she felt lost without the stimulating emotional charge of his presence. Apparently a good bit of the anger she was experiencing stemmed from missing him. Whatever her feelings—and they were clearly quite tangled where he was concerned—she deeply regretted advising him to get a mistress. It's the last thing I want him to do, she admitted to herself. Of course he probably has one already. Maybe even several. And no intention of discarding them in my favor. From the vantage point of her new life in Japan, she began to realize fully what kind of sacrifice she'd agreed to make.

It was still too early in Seattle to phone Maggie's physician and check on her progress. With nothing else to do, Nora went outside and walked the garden paths Seiji had introduced her to the night before. The chirp of birdsong and gurgle of water, the rustle of bamboo and the breeze singing in the pines calmed her a little. I'll have to make a life for myself here, at least temporarily, she thought. One separate and apart from Seiji. Once our vows have been spoken and we've engaged in the night of sex I promised him, I'll need something to do while I serve the rest of my sentence.

His mother relayed a message from him as they sat down to lunch—a sparing meal of tea, rice and broiled fish accompanied by some sort of pickle. "Before he left, Seiji asked that I teach you what's required of a Japanese wife, so you'll be able to perform your duties," Aiko said.

To her dismay, Nora learned she'd be expected to bathe Seiji every night that he was in Kyoto, not just scrub his back now and then. She'd also be required to make tea for him in the morning and help him dress. She'd pour his sake in the evening and pack a box lunch or *bento* for him every morning. In other words, she'd cater to his every wish.

"Of course we have people to cook," Aiko went on, in a tone that made it plain Jerrold Braet's Japanese descendants were as well or better off than their American counterparts. "But it's traditional that you pack your husband's lunch, make special meals for him now and then. If you wish, I'll teach you what I know about proper Japanese cuisine."

It was a generous offer, considering the older

woman's likely opinion of her. She doesn't have a clue what kind of marriage ours will be, Nora realized. If she did, she wouldn't give me the time of day, let alone offer me cooking lessons. Meanwhile, though Seiji had told her something about what would be expected of her, his mother was making it sound as if she'd be little better than a glorified household servant. I'm facing a night of sex with a man I don't want to want, followed by a year of servitude and humiliation, she realized.

A moment later, Aiko was asking whether any of Nora's family members planned to attend the wedding ceremony. It was a touchy subject and Nora tried to tread lightly. Having expressed horror over what she was about to do, though it would save the family department-store chain for his desperately ill sister's sake, her father and his third wife, Alison, planned to keep their distance. So did both of Nora's sisters, who by now were arguing that she'd gone too far.

"My Aunt Maggie, who's fighting cancer, would come if she were well enough," Nora said truthfully. "When I told her I was going to marry Seiji, she said it was time the separate branches of our family forgave each other. As you may know, my mother died when I was fifteen. As for my father and my sisters…" She shrugged. "I can't really count on them."

Aiko nodded sagely as if she'd expected as much. "Tomorrow the kimono-maker will come to measure you…bring fabric samples," she announced. "You'll need a wedding outfit, plus several other kimonos for special occasions. You'll find them quite comfortable. I see Seiji warned you about taking off your shoes before entering the house. I plan to order you several pairs of matching slippers."

* * *

Without Seiji, who didn't bother to phone, the evening was an uneventful one. The following day, the kimono-maker visited, spreading gorgeous lengths of plain, heavy silk and colorful brocade, patterned in motifs of cranes, butterflies, chrysanthemums and bamboo lattices, around the *zashiki,* all the while chattering to Aiko in his native tongue.

"He says you're very tall...that you would tower over most husbands," the older woman translated at one point, giving Nora a subtly disparaging look.

Though Nora touched some of the brocades, too, admiring their beauty, it was clear to her she was expected to defer to her prospective mother-in-law's judgment when it came to choosing any of them.

After much conversation in Japanese and the fingering of fabric lengths, Aiko turned to her. "I have selected the heavy white silk for your wedding kimono," she announced, gesturing at a bolt of smooth, densely woven fabric. "It will be lined and trimmed with red and have a matching headpiece. As for your special-occasion outfits, I have chosen the golden chrysanthemums and the green brocade with cranes. Also the dark blue with swirls and tiny lanterns in its design."

Unwilling to become a cipher in fulfilling the bargain she'd made with Seiji, Nora decided she wanted some input. "You've made several excellent choices, Mrs. Amundsen," she said. "In addition to them, I'd like something made from that pale aqua silk with a woven pattern featuring birds of prey. Given Seiji's interest in falconry, I have a feeling he'll approve. Naturally I'll be glad to pay for it along with your other selections."

Aiko gave her an offended look. "Seiji has instructed me that *he* will pay for whatever you need, since your father has refused to take any interest in your marriage preparations,'' she insisted. ''I'll add the aqua brocade to the list. Now, if you'll stand up straight and refrain from moving, Mr. Yamamoto will take your measurements.''

Early that evening, with the assistance of Michiko, who assembled the ingredients, Aiko summoned Nora to the table where they'd eaten the night before and gave her a high-handed, somewhat impatient lesson in how to prepare one of her son's favorite foods. They'd cook the dish, called *kai to yasai no yose-nabe,* over the gas burner. It would contain tofu, ginko nuts, shellfish, mushrooms and elaborate little cabbage rolls that had to be made from scratch.

No wizard in the kitchen under the best of circumstances, Nora rarely attempted anything more complicated than a cheeseburger. As a result, she found the recipe and the techniques necessary to produce it fairly difficult. Her obvious ineptitude as a cook had Aiko shaking her head.

That evening, as he sat alone in his luxurious hotel suite gazing out at Singapore harbor, which was dotted with freighters from the four corners of the globe, Seiji began to have second thoughts. Though he didn't regret his bargain with Nora and in fact considered its revenge component completely justified, he wasn't comfortable with the way he'd treated her the night before.

I shouldn't have left her alone with my mother so soon, he thought regretfully. *Or flown out of the country without saying goodbye. She probably feels abandoned...thoroughly disoriented.*

On impulse, he picked up the phone.

After a brief exchange with Aiko, who reported on

the kimono-maker's visit and his bride-to-be's obvious deficiency as a cook, he asked her to put Nora on the line.

"Is everything all right?" he asked, a hint of uncertainty reverberating in his voice when Nora said hello. "How are you and my mother getting along?"

In her brightest, most uncaring tone, Nora assured him she and Aiko were hitting it off famously.

Aware of his mother's deep-seated shock and resentment that he should choose a wife from among their hated American relatives, he didn't believe her. Either Nora's as dense as a bamboo thicket or she isn't leveling with me, he thought. And I doubt if it's the former. Mentally she's right on target.

Whereas physically...

Leaning back in his chair, Seiji pictured Nora's expressive face, her beautiful breasts and smooth, white shoulders. He imagined how it would feel to be deep inside her, with her long, shapely legs wrapped around him. Damn her, he thought feelingly. She's getting under my skin. Maybe I shouldn't have put her through that "bathing lesson." I could have taught her what to do myself, in privacy, once we were wed. With no humiliation involved and nothing off limits between us, it would have been far more pleasurable.

The recollection that, according to the terms of their agreement, those limits would be relaxed on only one occasion, was like running into a brick wall. Later, as he lay in bed gazing out at the city lights, he wondered if he'd finally made the mistake of caring about someone who had no real interest in him.

Abruptly he decided to go home early.

Chapter Seven

Two days later, Aiko came down with one of her migraine headaches, freeing Nora to do as she pleased for a few hours, as the servants could look after her prospective mother-in-law. Eager to see more of Kyoto, she asked Michiko—with the help of her Japanese phrase book and hand gestures—to phone for a taxi that would take her to the nearest city bus line. The last thing she wanted was to see the sights from the cocoon of Seiji's limousine and have his driver report her every move to him.

Purchasing a green-and-white, all-day bus pass for six hundred yen, she began her explorations, getting off wherever the spirit moved her. In the process, she visited Ryoan-ji Temple, with its austere garden of raked sand and carefully positioned stones, the treasure trove of the Kyoto Craft Center and Nishijin, the city's ancient textile district. Reluctantly heading back on the bus before Aiko started to worry, she spotted an outdoor market on Mishikikaji Street. Meanwhile, she was getting hungry. The fruit and vegetables displayed on a jumble of low tables looked positively delectable.

As she pulled the stop cord, she grinned at the thought that, in some ways, New York and Kyoto were similar. Each had plenty of colorful places to spend your loose change and poke around in a crowded, citified atmosphere.

The blended aromas of roasting tea and bread baking in ovens along the sidewalk were enticing, the fishy smells emanating from some of the stalls less so. Huge bouquets of chrysanthemums awaited purchase for beauty's sake along with tightly curled ferns and other exotic greens that were meant to be eaten, not displayed. The simple freedom to wander from stall to stall, admiring a pile of shiny orange persimmons here and purple eggplant there, in addition to purchasing several perfect peaches and a cellophane-wrapped carton of bing cherries, restored some of the lightness of her being. Thanks to the pull of Seiji's behavior on her emotions, it had all but deserted her.

She was in the process of attempting to talk herself into returning to the house when she overheard a slim, fiftyish Western woman speaking in Japanese to one of the stall-keepers. Though the woman's British accent was marked, even in the unfamiliar tongue, she was clearly fluent in the language.

When she'd completed her transaction, Nora introduced herself. "I can't help but admire your facility with Japanese," she said. "Though I'm fairly good with languages, it seems awfully difficult."

The woman, who gave her name as Rosemary Pennington, adding that she was the wife of a British diplomat, remembered Nora from a recent spread in *Vogue* magazine. "You're the model, aren't you?" she queried with a smile. "I thought I recognized you. Actually, Japanese isn't all that difficult if you tackle it phonetically and don't even *attempt* writing it."

She went on to explain that she'd been forced to learn the language in order to run her household and make basic conversation at social and diplomatic events. "Far from finding it burdensome, as I expected, I grew to like it and wanted to learn more," she admitted. "It proved to be very empowering. If you like, I'll give you the name of the language school I used. It's very efficient. They'll have you speaking with confidence...and understanding the replies...in just a few weeks."

Taking a small notebook out of her purse, Nora gratefully wrote down the school's name and address.

"Do you mind my asking what you're doing here, in Kyoto?" Rosemary Pennington went on. "A fashion layout, I suppose?"

Nora shook her head. "Actually I'm getting married."

The older woman's lively blue eyes twinkled with curiosity. "To someone who lives here? Anyone I might know?"

A bit diffidently because of her misgivings about the whole affair, Nora responded that her fiancé's name was Nels Amundsen.

"You don't mean *Seiji* Amundsen, surely?" Rosemary Pennington asked in surprise.

Nora nodded.

"He's a fairly powerful personality, isn't he?" the older woman said, complimenting her on her engagement ring. "We've met several times socially. He's rich as Croesus, or so I hear. All the women seem to be crazy about him."

Surprise and excitement hit Nora in the softest part of her stomach when she returned to the house to discover that her fiancé had come back from Singapore early. Still dressed in his dark, exquisitely tailored business suit, snowy white shirt and silk tie though he was wearing *tabi* on his feet, he'd been pacing the *zashiki* as he waited for her to appear. His tall, muscular frame seemed to fill the all-but-empty room, imprinting it with his personal force and magnetism. As he turned toward her, she caught a whiff of his aftershave.

What a spectacular man he is! she thought before she could stop herself. Exotic. Incredibly handsome. Possessed of his own internal power source. It would be so easy to forget the unfeeling limitations of our bargain and learn to care for him. The fleeting thought that he might greet her with a kiss, inserting his tongue into her mouth and pressing himself against her the way he had in her apartment on the night they'd met, aroused shivers of anticipation.

The angry expression on his face as he strode toward her doomed the surge of pleasure she felt.

"Where have you been?" he demanded, catching her by the wrist. "I thought you had..."

He let the words trail off as she freed herself.

Furious at the implied claim of ownership, not to mention his overbearing physical demeanor, Nora put some space between them. She gave him a pitying look as she rubbed the offended joint. "That I'd run the moment your back was turned?" she asked.

Her body language and the cutting tone she'd employed made Seiji feel like a fool, and he didn't respond in so many words. But then, he didn't have to. It was plain to both of them he'd thought *exactly* that. His shame was tinged with stubbornness and a reluctant appreciation of how lovely she looked with her green eyes flashing fury at him.

"You ought to know better," she added when he didn't speak. "I agreed to marry you to save Braet & Company for my aunt Maggie. And she's still alive, as far as I know. So we still have a deal. For your information, and *solely because I choose to tell you,* I was sight-seeing. Since I'll be living in Kyoto for a year, I thought I might as well get acquainted with it."

The implication, of course, was that all bets would be off if and when Maggie Braet succumbed to her illness. Nora was telling me the truth when she said she doesn't care about the company for its own sake. Or the wealth my shares will bestow on her, Seiji realized. She's made it clear that, for herself, she doesn't want anything to do with me, despite the sexual energy that crackles between us whenever we're together.

He refused even to consider the fact that she was beginning to matter to him. A past master at doing so, he hardened his heart even as he thought of a way to put her in her place.

"I've decided to move up our wedding ceremony to a week from Friday," he informed her blandly, as if he hadn't come to that decision seconds earlier. "Since we're having very few guests, and my mother informs me your wedding gown will be ready soon, that shouldn't pose a problem for anyone."

Nora knew it was probably clear from the shocked, rebellious look on her face that his arbitrary edict posed a problem for *her.* Though their marriage ceremony would be moved up by just a week, the fact that he hadn't bothered to consult her about it made her feel as if she were being ground into the *tatami* mat beneath his feet.

Apparently he's going to jerk my chain every time I surprise him with my independence or commit some infraction or other against his unstated code of behavior, she thought. If I'm to have any peace of mind at all during the next twelve months, I'll have to avoid butting heads with him. Still, she wasn't about to be anybody's dishrag. She'd promised him a night of sex and a year of marriage, and that was exactly what he'd get—not dominion over her every waking moment.

"Whatever you say," she responded in an icy tone. "As I'm sure you must realize, I'd prefer to discharge my obligation to you as quickly as possible."

The atmosphere at dinner that night was thick enough that Nora could have cut it with a knife. Discovering a streak of stubbornness in herself that would have astonished Stephanie with its vigor, she refused to meet Seiji's eyes or those of his mother unless it was absolutely necessary. She spoke only when she was spoken to, keeping her answers to a minimum. It was clear from the expression on Aiko's face that the older woman had begun to wonder what kind of marriage her son was contemplating.

Invited to join Seiji and his mother for a brief stroll in the garden after the meal was finished, Nora declined. "I've decided to turn in early, if no one has any objection," she murmured, daring her fiancé to insist she accompany them.

Concerned that Nora would reveal the terms of their agreement, he didn't push the point. Imagining for several heated seconds what he'd do if they were alone together, he found himself stymied even in his visualized scenario by the bargain they'd struck. She'd promised him a night of lovemaking. When it was over, his privileges would cease. Though their deal would satisfy his honor and avenge his mother's and grandmother's maltreatment, he'd long since realized a single night of sex with her wouldn't be enough.

Damn, he thought. I didn't earn my reputation as a tactician by allowing others to set my parameters. As he contemplated the standoff he faced once their marriage had been consummated, an idea began to take shape.

Following their clash the afternoon he returned from Singapore, Seiji and Nora stepped lightly in each other's presence. Though she'd braced herself for more "bathing lessons" and contests of will as their wedding day approached, none materialized. She got the uneasy feeling that he was planning something. Or waiting quietly for her to let down her guard. It occurred to her that he might be gentling her to the leash as he would one of his falcons. If the strategy worked, when she finally had freedom to roam, she'd be in the habit of returning to him.

I don't want to become attached to him that way, to *love* him without being loved in return, she thought, compulsively assessing the situation one night after everyone else in the house was fast sleep. Our engagement and marriage are just a means of retaliation to him. His heart will always be out of reach.

Their wedding day dawned cool and bright, with a hint of fall in the air. Before breakfast, so she wouldn't disturb Darien the moment she'd fallen asleep after a long, hard day at the hospital, she phoned Seattle for a progress report. Her spirits lifted at the sound of her sister's voice, doubly so when Darien told her Maggie was making progress.

"I never thought I'd be saying this," Darien admitted, "but she's rallied. I drove her home from the hospital yesterday afternoon, after hiring several people to take care of her in shifts. Of course, she'll have to continue her chemotherapy, which she hates because it makes her feel so tired and nauseous. She's also lost a lot of hair. But she's taking *that* in stride. The moment she heard she was being released, she phoned over to the flagship store and asked the home delivery people to send her a selection of wigs and turbans...the most stylish ones possible...even if they had to round them up at a competitor's."

Nora smiled in spite of herself. It sounded as if her sacrifice wouldn't be wasted. Maggie was fighting her cancer like a tiger. "How's everything going with the company?" she asked.

She could almost feel Darien's shrug.

"Pretty much the same, I guess," her sister answered. "Naturally Maggie's rabid to go back to work and straighten things out. Tell me...how are *you?* Sure you want to go through with this?"

Nora was torn, a good deal more ambivalent about marrying Seiji than she cared to admit, in part because of her unwilling attraction to him. "What choice do I have?" she answered as if they were discussing the price of her favorite ice cream at the supermarket. "Maggie's determined to get well so she can go back to running Braet & Company. After promising her the chain will be safe, I can hardly pull the rug out from under her."

Darien was silent a moment, as if listening to what Nora *hadn't* said. "You were always such an old softy," she declared at last. "Much as I love her, too, I don't think I could do what you're doing." She paused. "When did you say the wedding was going to be?"

Reluctant to divulge the extent to which she'd deferred to Seiji's high-handedness, Nora chose her words with care. "Actually it's this evening," she admitted, doing her best to suppress the little quaver that surfaced in her voice.

Darien couldn't hide her surprise. "What happened? I thought…"

"He decided to move up the date. I went along with the idea because the sooner his 'year of marriage' begins, the sooner I can return to my life in the U.S."

"I vote for that," Darien said heartily. "I feel so guilty for joining Steph in asking you to intercede with him, now that it's turned into such a big personal sacrifice. Still, I have to admit your assurances to Maggie have given her a boost."

Following their conversation, Nora spent most of her wedding day alone, eating little and obsessing about what the evening would bring as she wandered alone in the garden and sat quietly on a wooden bench half-hidden among the trees. From the time she'd been a young teenager, she'd regarded her virginity as a precious commodity that belonged to the man she'd marry someday. Now she'd had the temerity to place a price tag on it. Seiji Amundsen, as predatory as the raptors he trained for sport, would be its purchaser. The quaint, old-fashioned notion of love wouldn't play any part in their nuptials.

Finally it was time to dress. Ine, at fifty-something the household's senior female servant, came to Nora's room to help while Michiko, Shigeko, the kitchen maid, and the chauffeur's son, Yoshio, who worked part-time, arranged flowers and set out refreshments.

For Nora, putting on the traditional undergarments Ine handed her and then standing all but motionless as the servant helped her into her multilayered wedding kimono of heavy white silk faced with red was like a dream from which she expected to awaken at any moment. Even the servant's arrangement of her hair with special combs and careful placement of her kimono's intricate matching headpiece, known as a *kakushi* band, didn't make the process seem any more real to her. Instead of a bride eager to meet her groom, she was a stranger in a strange land, a woman standing at the brink of a precipice.

Too soon, the details were in place.

"You...very pretty, missus. Seiji-san like very much," Ine complimented in her halting, heavily accented English, which dated from her service to Jerrold Braet many years earlier. She held out a hand mirror for Nora's inspection.

I don't doubt for a moment that he will, given what these trappings symbolize, Nora thought, staring at her disembodied face. It seemed almost alien to her as it floated between her kimono and the exotic headdress.

She'd make it through the wedding if she could manage to regard it as just another modeling assignment, she supposed. Ditto what would come later, though that would be a lot more difficult. In Seiji's bed, she'd be fighting both the voluptuousness of his caresses and the incendiary effect of her own response to them.

Somehow, she managed a smile. "Thanks for everything," she whispered. "What am I supposed to do now?"

The older woman smiled, too, clearly mistaking Nora's mood for prewedding jitters. "Wait here," she answered. "I come back when is time. Here is fan. You hold when you come out, cover part of face. Is called *sensu*. This one special for weddings. Okay?''

Nora nodded. Her role was to stand deferentially at Seiji's side in front of the Shinto priest who'd marry them. She wouldn't have to say a word. Her presence would be consent enough. In case one of the guests spoke to her afterward, she'd armed herself with a stock response from her phrase book, the equivalent of ''Sorry, I don't speak Japanese. Do you speak English?''

With nowhere to sit unless she dragged one of the floor cushions out of the closet, crushing her gown in the process, she stood with folded hands in the middle of the mostly empty room, alone with her thoughts. Gradually the sounds made by arriving guests intruded. Their conversation gained in volume as someone began to pluck the strings of a *biwa* or Japanese lute. Any second now, Ine would return for her. Nervously she wet her lips. She couldn't stop herself from flinching when the servant reappeared.

''Is time, Nora-san,'' Ine said, beaming her approval. ''Seiji-san wait for you.''

He'd instructed her to enter the *zashiki* at Ine's cue and proceed to his side with downcast eyes and diminutive steps, the kind she rarely took, thanks to her fashion-model training and elegant, long legs.

''Think of the way Cio-Cio-San minces in her *geta* in *Madame Butterfly* and you'll have the picture,'' he'd suggested, the sardonic glint in his eyes all too evident.

The Shinto priest who'd marry them would stand with his back to the open *shoji* that offered a glimpse of the garden. Their guests, few enough to count on her fingers, or so she'd been told, would intrude only in her peripheral vision until after the ceremony.

A year of marriage will pass quickly enough, she tried to tell herself as she began to move. So will the night of lovemaking I promised him. By tomorrow, the worst will be over. I'll be able to concentrate on exploring Kyoto as I serve the rest of my sentence. She only hoped Seiji wouldn't keep her awake until dawn while he extracted the maximum benefit.

With a barely perceptible flicker of her lashes as she entered the *zashiki,* she took in her prospective mother-in-law's subtly disapproving face, the beaming knot of family servants, a more widely scattered complement of guests. All the men but Seiji were wearing business suits. As one of the ceremony's chief participants, he was clad in a black ceremonial kimono with a subtle geometric design and coordinating loose black trousers. Though she'd seen him in traditional Japanese garb before, the special clothing enhanced his air of being exotic, more than a little dangerous.

Everything about him attracts me, she realized to her dismay. He's a man in a million with that warrior build of his, those impassioned eyes and emphatic brows. When he ravages my mouth, boldly inserting his tongue, I want to open the innermost portals of my heart and soul to him. Even the way he uses his hands, the flare of his nostrils when he's tweaking my sensibilities, can turn my head.

Somehow, she had to save herself. Throw up emotional barricades faster than he could pull them down. Prevent herself from *loving* him. To feel that way about him when all he wanted from her was revenge would be the biggest mistake she could make.

As he watched her measured entrance, Seiji began to realize fully what an ironic situation he'd created for himself. Nora's celebrated good looks, her amazing spirit, the beguiling contrast between her glorious auburn hair and the Japanese wedding garments she wore so modestly but elegantly, would soon be his to exploit. So would her beautiful body with its satiny skin and light dusting of freckles. Could it be allowed to matter that the only thing she'd withhold from him, the generous and loving heart that had prompted her to make such a deeply personal sacrifice for her aunt's sake, was what he suddenly wanted most?

Held captive by arrogance and his reputation as the kind of man who controlled his own destiny, he didn't let his mobile, aquiline features betray what he felt. The last thing he wanted was for Nora to sense his eagerness. Or guess that it was bittersweet. Though his strongest emotions might be longing and regret, he'd keep to his plan, salvage as much satisfaction as he could from the bargain they'd struck.

When she reached his side, they bowed to each other, as arranged, and paid similar homage to the priest. Responding in kind, the stooped, elderly cleric began to recite their wedding service. To Nora, who couldn't understand a word, the formalities seemed to go on forever. Having eaten little for several days and even less since arising that morning, she was gradually overcome with dizziness. Her ears buzzing slightly, she felt herself swaying at one point.

Seiji promptly gripped her arm. "Are you all right?" his gaze demanded worriedly.

She nodded, getting hold of herself.

Abruptly the flow of words that would bind them together came to a halt. Nora realized they were now husband and wife. A slim platinum band nestled beside the diamond engagement ring he'd slipped on her finger the morning of their arrival. Responding once again to the priest's bow with deeper obeisance, they turned to face their wedding guests. Congratulations and wishes for long life and happiness were offered on every side.

Nora did her best to smile and nod as her new husband introduced her around, pausing at one point to explain in English that one couple lived just down the road from them. By now, sake was flowing freely. Seiji's chauffeur, who doubled as a man of all work, opened a chilled bottle of champagne and decanted it in Western-style tulip glasses.

"No alcohol for you until you've eaten something," Seiji decreed under his breath, leading Nora to one of the tables where Japanese-style hors d'oeuvres and sweets had been arranged on lacquered trays.

Unwilling to allow him to dictate her every move but aware, too, that her body's supply of fuel was running dangerously low, she consumed several sticky-rice balls coated with what Ine had told her earlier was red adzuki-bean paste. The surprisingly delicious little morsels helped restore her flagging spirits. I suppose I'll live through this, she decided, flashing her famous smile in response to several toasts as Seiji draped a possessive arm around her waist. A few years from now, it'll be as if I dreamed all this.

At last, having stayed the proper amount of time, the guests began to offer their final congratulations and depart. Joining Seiji and Nora to bid them goodbye, Aiko remarked in English to her son's chief financial officer, a Dane who was related to her late husband, that she finally had a daughter-in-law to care for her in her old age.

"I didn't think it would ever happen," she said with a laugh that sounded particularly mirthless.

She made several more pointed comments later, as she, Seiji and Nora shared a light repast.

"Don't let her get under your skin," Seiji advised after she had excused herself and retired for the night. "She'll accept you because she must. In her defense, it shouldn't be too surprising that, after a lifetime of being ostracized by her American relatives, she has unfriendly feelings toward them."

What am I supposed to say to that? Nora wondered. I agree. My family's treatment of her was incredibly shabby. And I'm paying a steep price for it. Shouldn't that be enough?

"I gather you haven't told her the truth about our bargain," she speculated.

His only response was a shrug. Silence lengthened between them like a slowly expelled breath. Meanwhile, the sun had set. The servants had retreated to their own quarters after lighting several old-fashioned oil lamps in lieu of switching on the harsher medium of electricity. Their mellow flicker was reflected in the dark pools of Seiji's pupils as he gazed at her across the table.

It won't be long now, she realized, absentmindedly tracing the pattern of her green silk kimono, which she'd donned in place of her elaborate, somewhat uncomfortable wedding dress. He'll suggest we go to bed. Undress me. Expect me to undress and bathe him. Ultimately we'll have sex. My virginity will be forfeit, like damages in a civil case. If she enjoyed what they did, once the pain everyone said was connected with a woman's first time had faded, she wasn't sure she'd be able to live with herself.

He didn't appear to be in any rush. "What do you

say we step outside for a moment before turning in?"
he suggested.

In response, she got to her feet.

Pausing on the *engawa,* a wooden platform beyond
the *shoji* that served as a kind of narrow porch, they
gazed up at the moon. Currently at the beginning of its
first quarter, it was little more than a pallid crescent.
While they'd been lingering over sake and dessert, a
nighttime chill had begun to pervade the air. The rocks
and trees, the stone lanterns and the little bamboo
sluice that fed the pond had reverted to darkened
shapes.

"Any regrets?" Seiji asked softly, gripping her
shoulders through her kimono's thin silk.

She granted him the liberty without protest. "If
you're asking whether I'd make the same choice if we
were discussing our bargain for the first time this evening," she admitted, "the answer's yes. But that
doesn't mean…"

He didn't give her a chance to finish the sentence.
Descending like a hawk falling from the sky onto its
chosen victim, his mouth claimed hers.

Chapter Eight

For the first time in their unorthodox relationship, Seiji pulled out all the stops, unleashing the prodigious sexuality she'd sensed in him. More assertive than his swooping appropriation of her mouth as she'd stood dripping and half-naked beside his friends' swimming pool, a thousand times more profound than the forthright claim he'd pressed when she'd arrived at his Vancouver condo, his fierce, deeply seeking kiss seemed to demand nothing less than the totality of her being, the very essence of her as a person.

Yet for a reason she couldn't fathom, it was also heartbreakingly generous.

I'll satisfy your every craving, he seemed to promise. *Excite your erogenous zones one by one until we both lose control, for as long as the liberty you've granted me remains in effect.* If she thought she'd misunderstood the offer, she had only to pay closer attention to the way he ran his hands down her back to grip her buttocks and position her more provocatively against him.

In that intimate embrace, the stirring of his desire was all too evident. God help me, she thought as she resonated to his touch in the deepest part of herself. I may not love him...yet. But I *want* him, so much that my insides ache with it. Half expecting him to undress her and ravage her on the spot, she almost stumbled when he drew back to hold her at arm's length.

"Much as I'd like to walk with you in the garden tonight, I've changed my mind," he said. "It's getting late. And we have other business to conduct."

Her cheeks flushing with embarrassment at the thought, she allowed him to lead her to his private bath. It was quickly apparent that one of his servants had preceded them. Fragrant steam rose in readiness from his big cedar tub. The bucket, dipper and other bath aids Michiko had used during her demonstration a week earlier had been placed near the drain for Nora's convenience.

The time had come to bathe her new husband.

"Michiko has put away your clothing and personal items in the closet and stepchest on the right," Seiji informed her matter-of-factly, gesturing toward his sleeping area. "It might be best if you hung up your pretty new kimono. It won't stay dry if you continue to wear it."

As he spoke, he casually removed his own garments and hung them on a peg on the wall, sat naked on the low stool. Modestly averting her eyes, Nora took his advice, placing her beautiful crane-patterned kimono on one of the padded satin hangers that had been provided. And paused. Why did they move everything in here, just for a single night? she wondered, a puzzled frown drawing her brows together. After tomorrow morning...

Abruptly she realized that, unfamiliar as they probably were with the terms of her bargain with Seiji, Aiko and the servants would expect her to share his room on a regular basis. Meanwhile, once their marriage was consummated, she didn't plan to sleep with him. She'd have to sneak in another futon for her personal use— make it a habit to bathe in the morning after he'd left for the office.

Returning to the tub area in her bra and panties, which were lacy and a bit more revealing than she might have wished, she scooped a pitcher of steaming water from the tub and poured it over him, following up with a second. A moment later, she was lathering his thick, dark hair with a hauntingly herbal-scented shampoo and firmly massaging his scalp with her fingertips.

It was far from the most titillating service she'd provide for him that evening. Yet his pleasure in it was obvious in his little grunts of satisfaction, the marked relaxation of his neck and shoulder muscles.

He commented on it, as well. "It's very pleasant, you know, having you touch me this way," he acknowledged in a low voice, reaching up to caress the curve of her hip and then running his hand down her thigh.

In response, she stepped back a little and poured another pitcher of water over his head. "You might want to close your eyes if you don't want to get soap in them," she suggested.

If they stung a little from her deliberate dousing, he didn't say so. "In remote areas of the countryside," he told her instead, his long, dark lashes sticking together in spikes, "there are still people poor enough that they can afford just a single tubful of hot water on any given evening, though there may be five or six people in the family. Naturally, the man of the house goes first. The lowest person on the totem pole, as you Americans like to put it, must wait to bathe until everyone else has finished and be content with their leftover bathwater. In most cases, that person is the daughter-in-law."

Nora had finished scrubbing his arms and chest, his powerful back muscles. She gave him a disparaging look. "That doesn't sound very sanitary. Or fetching, let alone liberated."

The quote marks deepened beside his mouth. "Luckily for you, I can afford to have as many tubs, as much hot water as I like. And I'm liberated enough to share mine with you. Of course, you'll have to scrub down, too, before getting in. That's traditional, in the interest of cleanliness. Though the husband doesn't usually scrub his wife, I'm willing to have a go at it."

The little flashes of humor that had passed between them hadn't blinded Nora to the fact that, if she agreed, it would be an invitation to touch her all over. But then, he'd do that anyway. She brushed a loose strand of hair back from her forehead. "Let me think about it," she requested.

She'd have to move forward with her work, sponge his hard, flat stomach and the area between his legs unless she wanted the bathwater to cool, their wedding night to lengthen into morning. Hesitantly she sank to her knees on the little waterproof pillow that had been placed nearby for her use.

He wouldn't let her avert her eyes from the task the way Michiko had. "Look at me, Nora," he insisted, gripping her chin and gently turning her head. "I'll be your first man if you've been honest with me. Don't you want to see how I'm made? Aren't you curious about the means of giving pleasure I'll put at your disposal?''

It was the last thing she'd ever have asked of him. Yet she was incredibly drawn to the notion. Opening her eyes as he'd instructed, she gazed at his jutting desire, the organs of generation that accompanied it. She'd seen unclothed males before, of course—in paintings and films. And stared at them with libidinous curiosity. Once during their high-school years, as summer campers in the Cascades, she and Stephanie had spied some boys their own age skinny-dipping.

None of these glimpses or clandestine sightings had prepared her for Seiji's masculine beauty. Her lips parting slightly, she picked up one of the more finely grained sponges and began washing him with it. A small, spontaneous movement on his part caused her to jump. Shivers raced up her arms in a thin glaze of excitement.

It's true what she told me...she's never done this sort of thing for a man before, he realized. I'm the first. ''Having you touch me there makes me want to make love with you,'' he admitted, laying a hand on her arm. ''Does it affect you that way, too?''

I don't have to answer that question, she shot back silently. Picking up one of the brushes again, she turned her attention to his thighs and calves, amazed at the firmness of his muscles.

At last, she was finished. Emulating the finale Michiko had demonstrated for her benefit, she scooped a fresh pitcher of water from the tub and poured it over him until the suds had disappeared. Inevitably some of the water splashed on her, causing the delicate fabric of her bra to become transparent.

Seiji's eyes narrowed as he watched. Getting to his feet, he made no move toward the tub. Instead he quietly repeated his offer.

I may as well agree to what he wants, Nora reasoned, declining to examine the gist of her logic too deeply. Whatever I say or do, he's going to undress me. Touch me. Invade my most closely guarded places. Shyly unhooking her bra, she hung it on a peg beside his things and turned to face him.

She'd never done nude shots for anyone, no matter how famous the photographer. Or stripped for any of her dates. "I suppose it would be all right if you scrubbed my back," she said, keenly aware of her own partial nakedness.

Damn but she's beautiful, Seiji thought in consternation. Her breasts are so lush. And rounded. An absolutely perfect shape. And her nipples...pink as a Titian nude's. He wanted to lick them. Imagine her with a child of his making sucking milk from her body.

He didn't have any right to linger over such thoughts. Theirs wasn't a marriage in the usual sense, more of a quid pro quo business arrangement. Even the fact that such a notion had occurred to him wasn't characteristic. He couldn't remember fantasizing about getting a woman pregnant.

Fetching a pitcher of water from the tub, he poured it over her shoulders. Unlike him, Nora declined to sit while he worked on her. Cursed with a back that always wanted to be scratched and rubbed, preferably by someone with tireless fingers, she relaxed enough to enjoy the light, impersonal but sufficiently lengthy massage he administered as he applied a soft-bristled brush to her lumbar region and the area between her shoulder blades. Still, she knew her reprieve from sensuality was a temporary one.

"Time to turn around," he said finally.

Biting her lip, she complied.

"Do you have any idea how lovely you are?" he asked, exchanging the brush for a sponge and wringing it out in the bucket of soapy water. "I don't suppose you do, despite all the adulation and publicity that's been heaped on your head."

In the short time they'd known each other, she'd been uncomfortably aware of his passion, which seemed ready to burst its bounds at the slightest provocation. But she'd never known he could speak or behave so tenderly. Each stroke of the sponge against her upturned peaks was as light as the graze of a butterfly's wing, yet so ardent it telegraphed messages of need to her deepest places.

Somehow, Seiji got hold of himself. He didn't stoop to rest his cheek against her forehead as he caressed her in that once-removed fashion. Or substitute his fingertips for the sponge's delicate strokes. Though it would be more difficult than any sacrifice he'd ever asked of himself, he'd keep to the plan he'd formed after their clash on his return from Singapore. That meant going just so far. And no further. It would be a supreme test of will, the samurai strength he'd inherited from his Japanese forebears.

An ironic smile tugged briefly at the corners of his mouth. I'll need the Viking toughness of my Scandinavian ancestors, too, if I'm to prevail in this, he thought. Maybe even Jerrold Braet's miscreant nerve. He's the one who got us into this predicament.

"Take off your panties," he urged Nora. "You won't be able to wear them in the tub anyway."

Her pupils swallowing the green of her irises, she did as he asked. Contrary to her expectations, his attention to her nest of auburn curls and the moist privacy between her legs was perfunctory, consisting of little more than a few strokes of the sponge. Seemingly eager to finish bathing her and get on with his soak, he moved lower to do her legs and feet, completing the task with a bucket of hot water, carefully poured over her shoulders so that her hair wasn't inundated.

"Time to get in the tub," he advised.

Maybe he planned to make love to her in the water. Aroused as she was by the thought of sharing that kind of intimacy with him, Nora doubted her inexperience would be a very good match for the gymnastics it might entail. A moment later, she realized she didn't have anything to worry about, at least for the moment. Waving her to a seat on one side of the tub, Seiji took one across from her. Their knees didn't touch. Lustful viewing was out of the question. The warm, herbal-scented water came up to their necks.

With a sigh that spoke of relaxation, not passion, Seiji shut his eyes. Left to her own devices, Nora found herself focusing on his face. Though the influence of his Japanese heritage was slight, she decided that Aiko and her mother, Yukiko, had bequeathed him their Oriental talent for inscrutability. When he wanted to, it seemed, he was able to hide all but his most unruly emotions.

Though it took a while, the water eventually cooled. "I suppose we'd better dry off, get ready for bed," Seiji remarked at last, opening his eyes.

Her feeling of awkwardness returning tenfold, Nora

tried not to watch him do likewise as she dried herself with an oversize towel. Finished, he tossed their towels into a bamboo hamper and flipped a switch, throwing the bath area into darkness. Motioning her to precede him up the three broad but shallow steps that led to the bedroom level, he closed off the bath behind them by drawing a pair of sliding *fusuma* together.

Even if someone came in to clean up after them, their privacy would be assured. However, it didn't appear that they'd consummate their marriage under cover of darkness. Though he snuffed out several of the oil lamps that lit the room, he didn't touch the one that illuminated the area of his futon from its position on a low table.

More vulnerable-feeling than ever as a result of her nakedness, Nora started toward the stepchest where her things had been put away to look for a nightgown.

At once a firm hand caught her by the shoulder. "No wife of mine is going to wear clothes to bed while I have the strength to prevent it," Seiji declared.

Nora's lower lip quivered despite her efforts to seem equal to the situation. "At least turn out the light," she whispered.

He gave her an incredulous look. "Why, when we've already seen and touched each other? Don't forget...this is our wedding night."

Her sense of defenselessness increased. Yet she knew his attitude was justified. The time had come to pay for Braet & Company's reprieve, her aunt's unexpected opportunity to have another go at living. She couldn't turn tail and retreat. Meekly, though a part of her chafed at his high-handedness, she returned to the futon and lay down on the side furthest from the garden entrance, with one of his hard, cylindrical pillows supporting her neck. She didn't attempt to touch the quilt they'd probably use later to defend against the night chill. If she tried to pull it up, she guessed, he'd stage another protest.

After taking a moment to gaze his fill, Seiji lay down beside her. This will be one of the hardest things I ever have to do, he thought. I hope I'm equal to it.

Thrusting one muscular leg between her thighs, he covered her partway and kissed her mouth, then lowered his head to suck lustily at one of her pink, upturned nipples. At once her other nipple stood erect, demanding similar attention. As if they'd always known the way, the passionate sensations he was evoking raced with the speed of light to the place where she wanted him most.

Aware from her helpless little gasps that he'd brought her unwilling pleasure, Seiji moved to suck at her other breast, then casually traced an uneven path of kisses down her stomach, stopping just short of the spot where she was on fire with wanting him.

A featherlight touch with one fingertip told him she was wet with longing for him, despite her virgin state and the aloofness she'd maintained earlier. About to break down and enter her despite his carefully laid plans, he hesitated. If I do this now, my bridges will all be burned, he reminded himself. I'll have used up the one chance I have to make love to her. If only I hadn't agreed to settle for a single night in her arms....

With an effort born of his strong will and lifelong desire to emerge a winner in everything he undertook, he quelled his passion. A moment later, he released Nora and blew out the lamp.

"Wh...what's wrong?" she stammered, still in the full flood of arousal.

"It seems I'm not in the mood tonight, darling," he replied with heavy irony, aware the words were something of an Anglo-American joke. "The fact is, I have a headache."

Positioning himself with his back to her, he appeared to go straight to sleep. Left lying there to stare at the ceiling in the dark, Nora was stunned, overwrought and frustrated. Has he no feelings? No decency? she asked herself. Or is this just another aspect of the revenge he's planned against the Braets...part and parcel of the humiliation I'll have to suffer for my aunt's sake? It crossed her mind that he might actually be hoping she'd leave, violating their agreement and letting him off the hook.

Whatever his motives—and she could think of several that would confound and humiliate her—she finally managed to fall asleep around 1:45 a.m., only to awaken some four and a half hours later at the shrill buzzing of Seiji's alarm. Without thinking, she sat up straight, then pulled up the quilt to cover herself. For the first time ever, there'd be a man in bed with her.

There wasn't.

Already dressed in an impeccably tailored suit, exquisite, handmade shirt and Italian silk tie, Seiji stood gazing down at her with a difficult-to-read expression on his face. "The successful businessman must get up early if he wants to beat the competition," he said, as if he were coaching a slow student.

A glance at his digital alarm, which rested on the low table beside the futon they'd shared, told her it wasn't quite 7:00 a.m. "You're going to work today?" she asked in disbelief.

He shrugged. "Why not?"

It seemed a honeymoon wasn't in the cards. Well, it

didn't matter to her. They were hardly newlyweds in the usual sense.

"Luckily for me, a successful model who's taken a year's leave of absence from her work needn't get up at this hour," she answered, her green eyes narrowing as she gazed up at him.

The smile that played around the corners of his mouth hinted he was one step ahead of her. "If that model happens to be you, she does," he said. "In Japan, married women have certain responsibilities. Like me, you're expected to join my mother for breakfast at seven if we're in residence. By then, of course, you'll have already packed my *bento,* or box lunch."

The duty of preparing his noonday meal rang a bell. According to the timeframe he'd quoted, she had just thirteen minutes to carry it out. Throwing back the quilt and giving him an unwilling eyeful in the process, Nora raced to the closet where her things had been put away and snatched up a *yukata* she'd worn several times since arriving in Kyoto. Not bothering to put on bra and panties, she lapped its front closed and fastened its sash firmly around her waist.

"Left front over right," Seiji instructed with a barely concealed smile. "Right over left is reserved for the deceased in a burial service."

Rolling her eyes, as much over his seeming delight in her mistake as over the impenetrability of Japanese custom, Nora righted the error and hurried off to the kitchen, where Shigeko was assembling pickled plum, miso soup with dried seaweed and raw egg, bowls of white rice and a pot of green tea for their breakfast.

She didn't speak a word of English.

"Bento?" Nora asked, making a question of it.

Smiling, Shigeko produced the traditional lunch container, a double-layered, round lacquered box with covers for each layer and a stiff carrying handle.

Lacking the faintest notion of what she was supposed to put inside it, Nora ducked into the Amundsens' tiny pantry. The sort of noncook who could ruin a TV dinner without half trying, she eyed the foreign-looking array of cans, boxes and cellophane-wrapped packages that lined its shelves. Even the printed illustrations that proclaimed their contents looked exotic to her. The *kanji* characters that accompanied them didn't help.

To her chagrin, the only things she recognized at first glance were rice crackers, a package of croissants, a tin of sardines and what appeared to be a can of tomato paste. In desperation, she made Seiji a sardine-and-tomato-paste sandwich using one of the croissants. Some loose rice crackers and a banana went into the box for good measure.

She presented her offering to him at the breakfast table with downcast eyes, keenly aware that—behind the lack of expression in his keen, gray eyes—he was probably laughing at her. I made a fool of myself last night, she thought, letting him get me hot and bothered that way. Well, it won't happen again if I can help it.

Watching her with his peripheral vision as he made some negligent comment or other to Aiko, Seiji picked up at once on her rebelliousness. I'm on the verge of feeling sorry about the way I treated her, he admitted to himself. But I'm not quite there. If I can build up her longing to the point where she's thoroughly frustrated by her need for me, yet refrain from actually consummating our marriage, maybe she won't limit us to a single night of pleasure. Of course, he knew that kind of waiting would take its toll on him as well.

The next few days brought a partial standoff. Though Nora bathed her new husband as before, there were no more amorous incidents. Shigeko went back to packing his box lunches at his request. Though the breather helped Nora relax a little, she continued to be on her guard whenever they were alone together. In part, she realized, that was because he refused to let her wear a nightgown to bed or sleep separately from him, yet made no romantic moves in her direction.

I want my part of our bargain over and done with, she raged as she paced in the garden one afternoon. Having it hang over my head like the sword of Damocles is more than I can take. Unfortunately, each time she engaged in that kind of reflection, the small but scrupulous voice of her own honesty contradicted her. Get real, Nora Braet, it prodded. You know you want what he hasn't offered you yet for its own sake. His unexpected reluctance to consummate your marriage is driving you crazy.

She was about to move toward closure herself when, a week after their wedding, Seiji announced he was leaving on another business trip. This time, he'd visit China and Vietnam to investigate investment opportunities there. He'd be gone for at least three weeks.

To Nora's dismay, on the morning of his departure, he gave her a provocative, seemingly endless goodbye kiss before getting into the back seat of his limousine for the trip to the airport. Memories of his fingers gripping her arms and his tongue passionately invading her mouth had already begun to haunt her as he disappeared down the driveway.

Chapter Nine

Nora used the time Seiji was away to avail herself of daily, rapid-immersion lessons in Japanese at the language school Rosemary Pennington had recommended. The lessons consumed six hours a day, five days a week, with a break for lunch. Thanks to the natural proficiency that had allowed her to learn Latin, Spanish, French and a modicum of German with ease, she was soon able to form simple sentences and ask for basic directions—understand most of the answers. Bit by bit, she found herself picking up some of Aiko's exchanges with the servants and their dialogue with each other, as well.

During her free time, she shopped for kimonos and other traditional items to give Darien, Stephanie, her father, her aunt Maggie and her agent for Christmas, as well as exploring many of the city's art museums and temples. For some reason, though it wasn't far from Seiji's house, each time she planned a trip to Kinkakuji Temple, one of Kyoto's most famous landmarks, something came up to prevent it. Then a shopgirl mentioned that the temple grounds were at their best when the autumn colors were at their most brilliant and she decided to wait a week or so. Maybe she could talk Seiji into accompanying her.

As before, he returned without warning a few days early. Handsome as ever and so sexy that just the sight of him tugged at her heartstrings, he was seated on one of the floor cushions in a *yukata* and loose trousers, talking with Aiko as she arranged flowers for the *tokonama* or decorative niche in the living area when Nora returned from her travels one afternoon.

Dressed in aloe green wool gabardine slacks and a matching sweater set as she entered the *zashiki*, she was carrying her shoes in her hands the way a young girl might carry her lunchbox. Her auburn hair was loose in a halo around her shoulders.

This time, Seiji didn't lose his temper over the fact that she hadn't been there, the epitome of a traditional wife, to greet him. Yet he couldn't seem to refrain from questioning her. "Where've you been this afternoon?" he asked, keeping his voice as even and nonconfrontational as he could make it.

For some reason, she didn't want to tell him about her sessions at the language school. "Shopping," she answered, adopting an indifferent air to mask the powerful tug of attraction she felt.

It was clear from Aiko's furrowed brow and pursed lips that she didn't approve of the offhand way Nora had answered him.

For his part, Seiji had vowed not to get upset with her. Still, his gray eyes glittered. "You don't have any packages," he said pointly, getting to his feet.

She shrugged. "I'm hard to please, I guess."

Chosen at random, the words seemed to reverberate with a hidden meaning. Was she trying to tell him he hadn't made the cut? Well, he'd see about that! Night after night, when he'd returned to his hotel room after a hard day spent conferring with industrial managers and party officials, he'd thought of her. Though female companionship had been readily available to him, he'd been thoroughly lacking in interest. There was only one feminine form he longed to clasp, one willful, liberated woman he wanted.

She didn't appear to want him. Plan or no plan, he decided on the spur of the moment that he'd waited long enough.

"Come with me," he demanded, catching her by the hand. "There's something private I want to discuss."

Nora went hot and cold all over when she realized he was leading her toward the bedroom they shared, in broad daylight. What would Aiko think?

"Why can't we talk in the garden instead?" she protested.

Very quickly, it became evident that she might as well have saved her breath.

"I'm tired from my travels," he muttered, tightening his hold on her arm as he slid the *fusuma* shut behind them, then released her momentarily to drag the futon they shared from the closet. "I want to lie down and rest with my wife beside me. I'm a married man. It's my right. And privilege."

Sleep was the last thing he wanted. And she knew it. By now, the entire household had probably guessed his intent.

Her cheeks burned. "You don't *have* a wife," she snapped back, resting her hands belligerently on her hips as he spread the thick cotton batting on the floor.

"Ours isn't a legal marriage, since it hasn't been consummated. I have absolutely no obligation to lie down with you."

The futon in place, he gripped her by the shoulders. *"That situation can be rectified easily enough."*

Though she struggled to free herself, Seiji pulled off her cardigan and dragged its matching shell over her head. Her bra came next, separating at its front clasp and falling to the floor under the passionate assault of his fingers.

"Your breasts are so beautiful I want to eat them for my lunch," he whispered, sweeping her off her feet so that her fullness was on a level with his mouth. "Not to mention my dinner and breakfast."

To her shock and fascination, he began to suck brazenly at one of her nipples. Sharp flickers of arousal raced down neural pathways they'd blazed on their wedding night, touching off bonfires of need in her deepest places. *Yes...oh yes!* she longed to shout. *This is what I've wanted from the moment I looked into your eyes beside that New York runway.*

Ablaze with the unexpected ferocity of her response, Seiji sucked possessively at her other breast, then returned her to her feet to caress both aroused peaks with his fingertips. "Take off the rest of your clothes," he coaxed, adopting the tone of a lover, not a despot. "I want to kiss you all over."

By now, Nora was in a state of meltdown. "I will if you will," she promised in a passion-muffled voice, fumbling with her slacks' waistband buttons and zipper tab.

The evidence of his need was burgeoning beneath his trousers. Flinging off his *yukata*, he unfastened them and let them fall, baring himself to her gaze.

"Touch me," he said with narrowed eyes. "I want to feel your fingers there."

Her lips parted, her breath coming in soft little gasps, Nora let him place her hand on the shaft of his desire. Abruptly there was no future for her, no past—just the moment in which they found themselves. With breakneck abandon, it invited them to ravish each other.

"You've said I'm beautiful," she whispered, stroking him, amazed such rigidity could be velvet to the touch. "Well, you're the beautiful one. I never dreamed a man could make me want him so much."

Her artless confession caused the last of their barriers to tumble. "Lie down and spread your legs for me, sweetheart," he urged, his beautiful eyes as torrid as red-hot ingots.

It was the first endearment he'd used that hadn't carried a heavy load of superiority or sarcasm. Shedding her bikini panties along with the last of her inhibitions, Nora did as he asked. The *shoji* to the garden had been left open a crack and the resulting shaft of sunlight illuminated her where she lay. Her auburn hair and ivory skin seemed to gather radiance against the room's deepening shadows, the futon's murky indigo-print cover.

Despite her slenderness, she's as lush as a nude in an Impressionist painting, Seiji thought, his need for her skyrocketing at an exponential rate. Yet it wasn't just her looks, her sensual allure, that he craved. Temporarily, at least, the vengeance he'd sought had ceased to have any meaning for him. So had any notion of one-upmanship in their relationship. For the first time in his life as a man who usually got his way, he wanted a woman because of who, not what she was. With all the considerable vitality he possessed, he longed to taste her sweetness. Her stubbornness and independence. Make her feel what he felt.

Their lovemaking would be her first. He'd have to take it slow. Briefly postponing the moves he hoped would take them to paradise, he gazed into her wide, green eyes, savoring the responsibility that had fallen to him. A moment later, he'd positioned himself between her legs and parted her nest of curls. Lowering his head, he began to explore her delicate folds with his tongue.

Breathless at the degree of intimacy he required, Nora shuddered with pleasure as he located the nub of her desire and concentrated his attention there. Sensation flooded her, fanning out from what rapidly became the center of her universe. "Yes...oh yes..." she acknowledged in a muffled voice, only half aware the words had escaped her lips. "*Please...* I want you to..."

Inexorable in its flowering, the arousal he stirred rose to flutter at the threshold of her endurance. Rational thought became an impossibility. Any bid to temper her response, retreat from the annihilation of her separateness in a sea of delight, was quickly out of the question.

Abruptly the longing that had intensified since he'd retreated from making love to her on their wedding night concentrated in a single point of light and heat. Completely at its mercy, she felt herself tense and tighten. Release came suddenly in a kind of explosion. Waves of pleasure washed over her, their force causing her instinctively to arch away from the futon as she grappled with her feet for purchase.

Sheltering her in his embrace, Seiji mutely invited her to ride her orgasm to the limit. By now, his hands spanned her hips. His cheek was pillowed on the flat of her stomach.

Her fingers tangled in his thick, dark hair, Nora accepted his beneficence, letting it carry her away. At last, she quieted. A slowly ebbing veil of gooseflesh bathed her thighs as she quaffed the pleasure he'd given her to the last inexorable droplet.

It occurred to her that their marriage still hadn't been consummated. "Seiji," she whispered, suddenly burning to give him the kind of release that he'd given her. "You didn't..."

"I know." His voice was like sandpaper against silk. "I want you to savor..."

She interrupted him in a little rush. "I have. Oh, I have. Come into me..."

She hadn't uttered a word about obligation. Or satisfying the terms of their agreement. Incredibly her eagerness to contain him and bring him pleasure seemed as genuine as his wish to please her. By the wildest stretch of his imagination, Seiji couldn't picture himself refusing. Yet his concern for her was uppermost.

"Now that the time has come, I'm afraid of hurting you," he whispered.

The discovery that he cared what happened to her, if only for that fleeting, uncensored moment, pierced her to the quick. "There's no other way," she insisted, supporting her argument with the kind of forthright caresses that, previously, she'd only dreamed about initiating. "Supposedly the pain doesn't last."

Tempted beyond his ability to resist, Seiji covered her with his hard, muscular body. Seconds later, she could feel him thrusting at her portal.

"Deeper," she prodded, wrapping her legs around him as she immersed herself in the possibilities. "Do what's necessary. I want you as deep inside me as you can get."

With a flash of discomfort that was quickly over, her virginity was lost, consigned forever to the memory of her life in chrysalis. Meanwhile, Seiji had begun to move with the rhythm lovers had favored since the beginning of time, slowly at first but gaining in momentum, letting ripples of sensation spread to the limits of her being as he led her back to the place of arousal.

When Nora awoke, the room was dark. According to the glowing numerical display on Seiji's battery-operated alarm, which currently rested atop his *tansu* chest across the room from them, it was 8:00 p.m., well past the household's usual dinner hour. Apparently Aiko had eaten without dispatching a servant to summon them.

Beside her, the man who was now fully her husband was still asleep, his breathing soft and even, his lashes sweeping the hard planes of his upper cheeks like those of a schoolboy. During their second lovemaking, he'd taken her all the way with him, imparting a pleasure so implosive and limitless that it was different in kind as well as scope, an epiphany of communion that had carried her completely out of herself.

It struck her suddenly that neither of them had bothered to use protection. I could be carrying his child, she thought with a shiver of fascination mingled with entrapment. Though the chances were slight, given her cycle, it was an outside possibility. Having his baby would cement bonds we vowed would be only temporary, she realized. Whether or not we chose to remain together, we'd be forever tied to each other.

Emotionally the prospect excited her. Yet she was

painfully aware that her acceptance of the idea probably meant she was falling in love with him.

He doesn't love me, she reminded herself. Considerate as he was, no doubt it's probably still revenge with him. Yet he desired her. She knew that much. He might still, though his objective in bringing about her family's humiliation had been realized. It was anybody's guess how he'd react a week hence, let alone when the year of marriage they'd agreed upon had reached its limit.

As if he could sense at some level that her thoughts were troubled, Seiji opened his eyes. "Are you all right?" he asked.

Nora nodded without speaking.

"It's late," he said softly, rising on one elbow to gaze at her. "And we haven't had anything to eat. What do you say I buzz Shigeko and ask her to prepare some leftovers? We can have them delivered here...just like room service."

The terrain of their lovemaking was inscribed in his gaze, a detailed map of what they'd done that afternoon and would almost certainly do again before they went back to sleep. Though his memory of the way she'd cried out in the throes of passion, yet pleaded with him to continue, made her shy, it pleased her, too. Risky as it was, given the temporary nature of their commitment, she wanted to pursue their intimacy to the limit.

"That would be great," she answered, abruptly hungry. "I hope you won't object if I put on a *yukata*. I don't want to scandalize the servants."

Seiji's mouth curved as he contemplated their shared indiscretion. "You needn't make the effort if you don't want to," he told her negligently. "They're well aware of what was going on."

* * *

He didn't kiss Nora awake the following morning as she'd hoped he would, despite the fact that they'd made love twice more after demolishing Shigeko's cold repast. But he wasn't standing over her in a business suit, either. She opened her eyes to find him chafing his nakedness with a towel. His hair clung in damp points to his forehead.

Apparently he'd used the shower that occupied one corner of their private bathing area.

"You're going to work today?" she asked in surprise. "I thought you weren't expected back until Friday."

He shrugged. "The empire never sleeps. What about you? Did you sleep well?"

Her mouth curved slightly as she gave him a shy nod. In truth, she'd sunk into a more profound state of relaxation than she could remember.

"Sex has a way of doing that to a person," he said. "I gather you liked it. Though it's not part of our arrangement, I'm willing to oblige again, whenever you want."

Nora flushed. I wish he hadn't phrased it that way, as if I'm the only one who enjoyed it, she thought, pulling the quilt they'd shared up to her chin as she watched him put on his underwear, hand-tailored shirt and smoky gray suit. It isn't any secret that he did, too, despite his vast experience. He just wants to make sure that, if we continue as lovers, it'll be at my behest. That way, he won't have to give up his precious illusion of self-sufficiency.

That he'd penetrated *her* defenses—symbolically as well as otherwise—was a fact she had to accept. Though she had no clear idea whether he'd ever be within her reach, she was more than half in love with him.

The moment he left the room, she rose, took a quick shower and put on a kimono. No way was she going to let Aiko think she was embarrassed by what had taken place between her and Seiji the previous afternoon.

She made it to the breakfast table while he was still there, conversing with his mother. Bowing, she appropriated one of the floor cushions. Efficient as always, Michiko quickly provided the American cereal, skim milk, coffee and fresh fruit she preferred to rice, raw egg and soup.

Murmuring her thanks, Nora exchanged a fleeting glance with Seiji before lowering her eyes. Though he and his mother switched to English as a courtesy to her, the latter slipped back into Japanese for a question or two concerning household matters. Out of habit, perhaps, he answered her in the same tongue.

Glancing at Nora, Aiko suddenly changed the subject. It was clear from her body language that she was speaking about her new daughter-in-law.

"Though we live in the same house, I hardly know her yet," she complained, as if returning to a topic she hadn't finished discussing. "Does she treat you well? Are you *happy* with her?"

Seiji's response was brief and, for Nora, with her rudimentary grasp of the language, somewhat difficult to grasp.

A moment later, he was getting to his feet. Abandoning what remained of her breakfast, she excused herself as well and accompanied him to the house's front entrance. His chauffeur had already brought the limousine forward. It was parked and waiting, with its engine running, in the gravel turnaround.

"Did your mother ask how things were going between us?" she quizzed as he bent to slip on his shoes.

"How did you know?" he asked in surprise.

"I've been taking Japanese lessons. What did you tell her?"

His gray eyes glinted with amusement. "Just that the situation's well in hand."

Though she bathed him that evening in her capacity as a traditional Japanese wife, Nora didn't have to guard against her strokes becoming caresses despite his forthright sexiness. She declined his offer of a similar service. Too upset by his casually infuriating response to her question that morning to attend her classes, she'd been brooding about it for most of the afternoon. In her opinion, Seiji's offer to have sex whenever she wanted it was so much baloney, just another ploy on his part to gain the upper hand by placing her in the role of supplicant. She had no intention of confessing she desired him if he didn't plan to reciprocate.

He'd insisted she sleep nude and she didn't plan to argue the point, hoping it would arouse and frustrate him. Meanwhile, it was the Japanese equivalent of a balmy Indian-summer night—much too warm for the use of a heavy quilt. Yet that was what had been left tightly rolled-up at the foot end of their futon by one of the servants.

Apparently Seiji expects me to lie down naked beside him in the absence of anything appropriate with which to cover myself, she speculated. Determined not to fall victim to such a scheme, she produced a smooth percale double bedsheet patterned in zebra stripes from her *tansu* chest and tucked it into place.

"Where'd you get that?" he asked in surprise.

"Braet & Company," she answered, relishing what she considered a modest coup as she dropped her towel and dove beneath the item in question. "I asked one of my aunt's assistants to ship me some American-style linens before I left the States."

The man she'd married gave her an incredulous look. "As it happens, we have sheets in Japan, too," he informed her. "I was just going to suggest that we appropriate one from the linen cupboard."

Chapter Ten

Nora felt like a complete idiot. Of course they have bedsheets in Japan, she chastised herself. What did you expect? It's hardly a third-world country. Just because Seiji's so uncompromisingly traditional, with his *tatami* mats and bare rooms, his emphasis on preserving custom, doesn't mean everyone decorates their house that way. Or behaves as he does. It wouldn't surprise me if he goes to extremes as a way of compensating for my family's rejection of his female relatives.

If he and Aiko wanted to discuss her privately, she decided, she'd get over it. Ditto any false modesty she possessed. Seeing her naked night after night would bring about its own revenge—making the bargain they'd struck that much more difficult for him to keep. Unfortunately playing that kind of game with the first man who'd set her heart ablaze went against her nature.

For his part, Seiji was feeling his way in unfamiliar territory. Unlike Nora, he'd had his love affairs, his infatuations. And moved on, without jeopardizing his bachelor state. Now, with the better part of their "year of marriage" still ahead of them and the damages he'd extracted in lieu of ruining Braet & Company paid in full, he wasn't sure how to proceed. He only knew that he wanted the beautiful redheaded model he'd married in a formal Shinto ceremony with every scrap of libido he possessed.

If only we'd met some other way...that Jerrold's abandonment of his first wife and seduction of my grandmother weren't our only connection, he lamented. With his track record of romancing and discarding the women in his life, it didn't occur to him to ask what he would have done differently in that case.

Accordingly their standoff continued for several weeks. Then he got up from the futon they shared one weekday morning and decided not to put on a business suit. Instead he removed an off-white fisherman-knit sweater from his *tansu* chest and pulled it over his head, zipped up a pair of faded jeans that did wonderful things for his tall, muscular physique.

As he'd hoped, Nora's eyes held a question.

"Aren't you going to ask me what I have in mind?" he prodded.

She regarded him with her head tilted slightly to one side. "Okay. I'm asking," she said.

"I thought we might tour Kinkakuji Temple grounds. That is, if you're willing to cut your language classes. The weather's perfect."

Surprise and pleasure flooded her, sailing past the emotional barriers she'd erected. He'd volunteered to be her guide. He wanted them to spend time together.

"I'd like that a lot, Seiji," she answered.

"How about getting up and eating your American-style cereal, then? I'm planning to make some improvements to the garden. Before we go, I'd like your opinion about a couple of things.''

Throwing off the coverlet they'd shared, Nora unearthed loafers, thoroughly broken-in jeans of her own, a fine-gauge sweater set. The chance to consult with him about his landscaping project suited her perfectly. A lover of growing things, she'd always wanted a garden of her own, the opportunity to raise orchids. Yet she had to admit she was puzzled by his request. Plants take time to mature…gardens years to perfect, she reminded herself. If our bargain's to be played out to the finish as we constructed it, I won't be around to share the results of our discussion with him.

By the time they settled on floor cushions at the breakfast table, Aiko had finished eating. Wishing them a pleasant day, she retired to her private area of the house with the stated intention of catching up with the household accounts.

On their walk after breakfast, Seiji quizzed Nora about the relative merits of rhododendrons and azaleas, weeping cherry and *salix babylonica*. Did she like the scent of sweet olive? The twisted shape of Japanese black pine? Or the more upright habit of cedar? What about a massive planting of iris just there, where the pond would reflect its brilliance? He planned to import some boulders, construct a small waterfall.

The project consumed the better part of their morning. Though Seiji took some notes on Nora's comments and his own ideas in a small notebook, which he shoved into his hip pocket when they'd finished, he didn't voice any firm conclusions.

''Maybe we'll get some ideas at Kinkakuji,'' he said. ''Before we head in that direction, I'll take you to lunch. Try not to embarrass me by ordering sardines and tomato paste.''

To think she'd have the sexy, sought-after CEO of Amundsen International to herself for an entire afternoon. It was almost as if he were courting her. Though she didn't dare hope their relationship would be transformed by it into something tender that would last, the ordeal of bathing him every evening and sharing his bed while remaining physically separate from him was beginning to take its toll.

The rustic restaurant he'd chosen, which partly overhung a narrow, rushing stream, was situated well beyond Kyoto's northern suburbs. When she questioned its distance from his house and their destination of the afternoon, he told her it was immaterial. With a chauffeur at his beck and call, he could spend the travel time going over some plans for a new factory he planned to construct in Seoul, if he was so minded. As a matter of fact, he had them with him. They were in one of the limousine's leather seat pockets. Would she like to see them on their return trip?

Kinkakuji welcomed them, its extensive, subtly landscaped grounds ablaze with maples clad in gold and scarlet dress against a sober backdrop of pines. Tiny vivid star-shaped leaves rustled beneath their feet and drifted on the central pond like a scattering of baubles or carp flashing just below the surface.

The temple itself, a three-tier, pagoda-like structure that doubled in reflection, shone like the sun in its delicate armor of gold leaf. It reminded Nora of a ship in a fairy tale. Captivated as a child might have been, she imagined the upturned corners of its eaves lifting like sails in the breeze as it set forth on some chimerical journey.

They were so close she could feel Seiji's breath on her neck as he explained that the original temple, constructed on a site once occupied by aristocratic thirteenth-century villas, had been torched in 1955 by a crazed Buddhist priest and burned to the ground. It followed that the current building was a reproduction.

"If photographs don't lie, it's every bit as beautiful," he said softly, brushing a strand of hair back from Nora's forehead. "The incident was transformed into a novel by Yukio Mishima. I have a copy I'd be glad to lend you. Unfortunately it was printed in *kanji* characters."

When she'd looked her fill, they continued their leisurely stroll around the grounds, ultimately pausing on a small, humpbacked bridge to look back in the direction from whence they'd come. Once again, Seiji was standing very near and Nora couldn't think of a way to break the silence that suddenly enveloped them.

"I want more than anything to kiss you," he confessed at last, his beautiful eyes glittering with reflected sunlight. "Will you allow it? The physical part of our bargain has been satisfied. I can't claim the right by virtue of my status as your husband."

His unexpected deference swept past her defenses as no physical attempt to win her compliance could have done. In a gesture that tugged at his heartstrings, she placed her palms trustingly against his chest. "Surely you must know the answer's yes," she whispered.

In response, he bent to claim her mouth. The long, slow kiss they shared, there on the little bridge with several tourist couples and three giggling children brushing past them, was so profound, so utterly annihilating of their separateness, that Nora ached with it. I want to give him everything, she thought. Freely, without reservation. Possess him completely. Lose myself in making love to him.

It was neither the time nor the place to do anything of the sort. Drawing back, though he continued to imprison her in his arms, Seiji gazed down at her. "I've taken the liberty of arranging a weekend for several couples at my country home in the foothills of the Japanese Alps," he said at last. "There'll be a full moon, and I plan to hold a formal viewing. The panorama of sky and mountains from there is breathtaking. I hope you'll come with me. If you agree, we'll leave day after tomorrow...be gone several days."

She'd get to meet some of his friends. Spend time with him away from Aiko. See him work the falcons he kept. And participate in a revered Japanese pastime that focused on the moon's ripe beauty and the recitation of poetry. In a sense, it would be the honeymoon they'd missed.

"It sounds wonderful," she murmured, refusing to think of the changes a year could bring. "I'm game."

They returned to the limousine with their fingers laced together. Out of the corner of her eyes, Nora saw that Harumi, Seiji's chauffeur, had noticed it. Aiko will know at once that something has changed between us, she realized, even if our hands aren't clasped as we enter the house. Though she isn't privy to our bargain and its ramifications, she'll sense the difference.

That night, in the privacy of Seiji's big cedar tub, they came together like magnets. This time, to Nora's relief, he was equipped with protection. Touching, whispering, fitting themselves together with an urgency that was all the more erotic for the water's steaminess and the way they tried to muffle their movements, they ascended the heights and collapsed back into each other's embrace.

A reprise on his futon in a yellow circle of lamplight was slower, more subtle, yet every bit as soul-shatteringly complete. Afterward, though they both were spent, they couldn't seem to let go of each other.

"I hope you won't mind if I wake you from sleep when I've recovered my ability to perform," Seiji warned with narrowed eyes, blowing out the lamp. "Because I'm never going to get enough of this."

I could keep loving him all night, Nora thought, gazing up at him. Inexperienced as I was, I've developed an infinite capacity to be pleased by his lovemaking.

She had to face the fact that their love might be temporary. "Neither am I," she answered, relinquishing any attempt at control. "You know the way inside me. That'll be wake-up call enough."

Bound by the secret life they suddenly shared, they drove to Seiji's country house on Saturday morning. The sky was red when they left Kyoto. Nora yawned and covered her mouth, causing a flash of brilliance from the diamond she wore to ricochet in the first rays of sunlight as Seiji poured tea for himself and coffee for her in the limousine's back seat.

Little by little, they left urban Japan behind, accessing a countryside of farms and small villages with vegetable gardens, the occasional local shrine or patch of forest. Though unsightly telephone poles and their accompanying wires bracketed the highway, which ran beside a little stream, previously distant mountains seemed to move closer to them.

A series of turns on unpaved side roads that climbed steep hillsides clad in Japanese cedar brought them at last to the doorstep of Seiji's country retreat. Like some storied *ryokan* or travelers' inn dating from the nineteenth century, it had heavy, timbered walls. A steep, thatched roof sheltered it like an overcoat. The cottages and sheds connected with its owner's interest in falconry were visible at a distance.

"The place was a wreck when I bought it," Seiji remarked. "The roof was falling in. Bats lived among the rafters. The kitchen floor was beaten earth. Layers of soot covered everything."

Nora's first glimpse of the interior took her by surprise. Unlike the Kyoto house, his country abode had polished board floors, oriental rugs and sparingly arranged upholstered furniture. Yet the effect was astonishingly similar.

It's the ceiling height, she decided, gazing upward past soaring beams to the roof's neatly woven underside. You get the same sensation of limitlessness. Serenity was everywhere she cared to look. Yet she suspected passion could flower readily in such a place.

"Come out on the deck. There's a good view of the pond and the fields below it," Seiji invited as Harumi put away their things in the master suite.

The chauffeur, who doubled as a cook when his employer was in residence there, barely had time to stock the bar, put away the supplies they'd brought and prepare a light lunch before their guests began arriving. Clad in a plum-colored angora sweater that was cropped at her bottom rib and a matching corduroy miniskirt that made her famous legs seem to go on forever, Nora stood at Seiji's side to greet them.

Beaming as if to suggest he'd pulled off quite a coup in marrying her, he introduced her to the four men and three women he'd invited. All of the guests were shorter and darker than he, with marked Japanese features.

One of the men, who ran a world-famous company, and his wife, an artist, were in their early fifties. By contrast, another couple, Kawai and Haruko Nakanishi, both of whom worked for Seiji at Amundsen International, were in their thirties. Seiji commented that they were newlyweds. The two remaining men, in their thirties or early forties, were unmarried. One had brought his cousin, Tamao, a handsome, sophisticated-looking single woman who appeared to be in her late twenties. Plainly she and Seiji already knew each other.

When he introduced Tamao to Nora, she murmured that she'd seen the latter's picture in countless fashion magazines. As for herself, she added proudly, she worked as a broker on the Nikkei Stock Exchange.

After lunch, which was served al fresco, Seiji's falcon-master and his assistant, both of whom lived full-time on the property, brought a pair of hooded birds along with several hunting dogs to the terrace behind the house by prior arrangement, so he could demonstrate his skill with them.

The birds, one large and one small, were attached to the falconers' gloved hands by leather leashes that fastened to permanent bands around their ankles. The leashes were hung with what looked like miniature sleigh bells.

"If one of the birds decides to go AWOL, or gets lost or wounded, the bells make it easier for us to locate her," Seiji explained.

"Are they all female?" Nora asked in surprise.

"Actually, yes." His mouth curved. "They're the most ruthless, the best hunters because, in the wild, they have babies to feed and protect."

The larger of the two birds, he went on to explain, was a goshawk, the most popular breed of raptor in Japan. Unlike the smaller, a sparrow hawk he'd acquired in the States, the goshawk was apt to crash through the brush like a low-flying plane in pursuit of its prey. She'd fight it out on the ground with a pheasant, even attempt to follow a woodchuck into its hole.

"Whereas the sparrow hawk 'waits on' overhead, riding the thermals or warm-air currents while the hunter and his dog help flush the target, then strikes from above like a missile," Tamao supplied, making it clear to everyone present that she knew the ropes.

Irritation flickered in Seiji's eyes to be quickly hidden. "That's right," he acknowledged, putting on the ultraheavy leather glove one of his falconers handed him. "Before we release any game, I want to demonstrate for Nora's benefit how these birds are trained..."

Settling the larger bird on his wrist, he removed its hood. Nora gaped at its glaring, red eyes, which appeared to focus with quiet rage in her direction. "She looks so fierce. She won't suddenly fly up and peck off my nose, will she?" she said anxiously.

He shook his head. "Actually she's afraid of strange people, cats, any dog she doesn't know. Her perpetually angry look comes from the pronounced ridges on her forehead," he explained. "I trained her with an extralong leash and tidbits fastened to a bird-shaped lure before I gave her a taste of freedom. She gradually learned that, even when we're hunting wild animals, she's not supposed to demolish them. Or peck at humans, though she'd do so in a heartbeat if she had a nest to protect. If she does what she's told, she gets an easy lunch...hunks of raw beef dusted with bonemeal.

The same thing happens during a refresher course. Watch.''

Unclipping the bird's leash from the corresponding ring on his glove, Seiji tossed her into the air, letting her fly free until she was little more than a speck in the distance, then lured her back with a whistle and a treat supplied by one of his assistants. Quivering, the dogs settled back on their haunches, aware their services weren't required yet.

''So it's the food that brings her back to you,'' Nora said.

Seiji shrugged. ''That and habit. Most falconers claim their birds' minds are alien to humans. I happen to be of the opinion you can form a relationship with them...one in which they know who's boss.''

It was time for those guests who were so minded to try holding the birds and setting them free before calling them back to the lure. Skeptical of her ability to perform as indicated, Nora demurred. She climbed the stairs to the deck hoping to observe the proceedings quietly from above. To her chagrin, Tamao quickly joined her, commenting on the weather and passing along a tidbit of gossip about the male cousin who'd brought her.

Before long, she got around to her real purpose, as Nora had felt certain she would.

''I know it's not polite to ask, but was your marriage to Seiji arranged?'' she said in her perfect if heavily accented English.

Unwilling to discuss such a personal matter with a perfect stranger, Nora regarded her with a puzzled expression. ''I don't know what you're talking about.''

The woman wasn't to be put off so easily. ''Rumor has it your family arranged your nuptials as a way of saving its department-store chain from ruin,'' she persisted. ''Naturally everyone's curious.''

Let them be, Nora thought. ''Since you ask, the simple fact is that Seiji proposed and I accepted,'' she said.

''I'm sure Haruko Nakanishi will be interested to hear it,'' her interlocuter replied with a faintly disappointed half smile. ''No doubt you've heard she was Seiji's mistress before she married her husband, Kawai, last spring.''

It was clear to Nora that her husband and Haruko were still friendly. Though she got a sick feeling in the pit of her stomach imagining them together, she didn't let it show. ''What about you?'' she asked, with such casual equanimity that it seemed nothing could faze her. ''Were you his mistress, too?''

Swiftly hiding her surprise at such directness, Tamao nodded with a rueful smile. ''I was the one before Haruko.''

Seiji chose that supremely awkward moment to appear. He asked if he could talk Nora into changing her mind and letting one of the falcons fly from her fist. ''We needn't get into the blood and guts of hunting actual game if you don't want to,'' he persuaded.

Determined not to let on that she'd been given an unwelcome glimpse into his past or get stuck in a lengthy tête-à-tête with Tamao, she agreed to give it a try. To her surprise, she handled the smaller sparrow hawk very well.

I can understand better, now, how Seiji operates, she thought, as the hawk flew free, then returned at her call to devour the morsel of beef she offered it. He's grooming me the same way he grooms his hawks, so that I won't want to leave him when the time comes. Though she couldn't imagine herself remaining in Japan full-time for the rest of her life, she couldn't picture living without him in the U.S., either. Whatever happened at the end of their year together, it would be a wrench.

Meanwhile, she could feel her husband preen as several of the men flirted respectfully with her. It seemed her willingness to work the wild creature, along with the fact that she spoke a few words of Japanese, had duly impressed them.

Seiji's attentiveness throughout the long afternoon and later, as they'd rested and drunk Sapporo beer on the terrace, went a long way toward restoring Nora's equilibrium. Your marriage didn't begin as a love match, though from your perspective it might be headed in that direction, she acknowledged silently as Seiji made a toast to friendship. His flings with Haruko and Tamao are in the past. Tamao would have been only too happy to tell you if that weren't the case.

The moon viewing wouldn't begin until it was fully dark. In the meantime, they gathered for a light supper of local delicacies. Thanks to the help of an area woman who'd supplied some of the ingredients, Harumi had prepared an array of tender mountain greens, fish from the nearby river and lacy, tempura-fried vegetables. The potpourri of tastes was both subtle and exhilarating.

To Nora's relief, there'd be just five people present when they gazed at the moon and recited *haiku* in its praises. Since Seiji's country house was too small to accommodate everyone who'd spent the afternoon with them, neither the Nakanishis nor Tamao and her cousin had been invited to spend the night. It was a lengthy drive back to Kyoto. They'd be forced to depart before the moon viewing in order to arrive home at a decent hour.

When the meal was over, the four guests who'd be driving back bade them goodbye, bowing and offering their thanks for a delicious meal and a pleasant visit. Without Tamao and Haruko to remind her of her husband's former love life, Nora could feel herself relax by inches. She began to daydream about the private moments she and Seiji would share when they were alone together.

When the moon had risen fully, twinning itself in the pond, they changed into kimonos, carried floor cushions out onto the deck and settled in a semicircle facing the water. Harumi brought sake, distributing it in little cups. Somewhere an owl hooted. Though the night air was cool, the chirping of insects arose from the marsh, reminding them of the summer's bounty and autumn's contrariness.

For a while, nobody spoke. The moon seemed to float in its own effulgence as it trailed silver over the pond and its surrounding wetlands.

At last Seiji asked that Masamitsu Iriyama, the fifty-something executive officer of an internationally known company, begin the haiku recitation. Acknowledging the honor with a seated bow, the graying, bespectacled businessman chose a poem by the Japanese master Basho. Making the classical, subtle connection between two seemingly unrelated subjects, it juxtaposed autumn moonlight with a worm working its way into the creamy interior of a chestnut.

After a lengthy silence in which Nora knew everyone was expected to meditate on the moon and the poem's resonance, the CEO's wife, Kuniko, followed with a selection of her own. She chose a triplet by Issa that sung of a snail half naked in the moonlight.

The remaining guest, Toru Tanizaki, a gifted young architect who would design and supervise the building of a major new facility for Seiji in Denmark, chose a haiku by Buson, which focused on the irony that, by moonlight, a blossoming plum could be mistaken for a bare, snow-clad tree in winter.

Though Nora's grasp of the Japanese language was growing daily, she hadn't mastered its subtleties sufficiently to interpret poetry. Accordingly, after each brief recitation, Seiji translated in an undertone.

To her, the simple, three-line character of the poems seemed to spring from a bittersweet appreciation of paradox, beauty's transitory nature and the melancholy they evoked. They make me think of our year of marriage and what will likely be its too-swift passage, she acknowledged, covertly glancing in Seiji's direction.

At first she'd thought the twelve months she'd agreed to give him would last forever. Now, she feared they'd fly too quickly from her grasp. Before she knew it, she'd be back in New York. Divorced. Taking her turn on the runway. Her heart would ache like a stone in her chest.

I don't want to love him, she protested. He won't love me back. Yet a part of her knew it was too late to save herself.

It was Seiji's turn to contribute a poem and, to Nora's surprise, he composed one on the spot. "Moon's cold breath breathes silver gooseflesh on the pond. Old woman touching me," he said softly, speaking in English for her benefit.

Proper decorum dictated that Nora remain silent and let his poem resonate. Despite her curiosity, she was careful to observe it. Hence, it wasn't until after their guests had stirred and murmured their approval that she slipped her hand into his. "I didn't realize you were a poet as well as a businessman," she whispered. "That was lovely. Of course, I can't help wondering who the 'old woman' is."

"Actually, I was thinking of my grandmother, Yukiko Braet," he answered, matching her tone. "I wish she were still alive. Knowing you would have helped to ease her shame and hurt. She was much gentler in spirit than my mother is. I think you would have liked each other."

An hour or so later, after Nora had recited a haiku she'd memorized for the occasion and there'd been ample time for everyone to contribute again, they rose, bade their guests good-night and disappeared into the master suite.

Harumi had filled their tub. The steamy tile-and-cedar master bath was redolent with the herbal fragrance of some bright green, aromatic salts he'd flung into the bathwater.

Briefly letting go of Nora's hand, Seiji stripped off his kimono and hung it from a peg. The initial shyness she'd felt with him little more than a memory, she followed suit, offering him her nakedness.

He didn't hesitate to take it.

"Come here," he growled, his beautiful eyes getting their smoky look as he tugged her into his arms. "I've been wanting you since morning...so much that I'm burning up with it. The night isn't going to be long enough."

Chapter Eleven

Ultimately they slept, of course—tangled up in their exhaustion and the utter physical release their love-making had brought. In the morning, they were drowsing so deeply that Harumi had to wake them by tapping on the wooden frame of their *fusuma* and gently calling out their names. Their guests were up and dressed, awaiting breakfast, he told them. Besides, Seiji-san had mentioned he wanted to be back in Kyoto by midafternoon, in order to prepare for his trip to Taipei.

At the reminder, Seiji sat up, throwing off his half of the quilt that had covered them. "We'll be out in a few minutes," he promised in Japanese, the language Harumi had used to address them.

Rubbing the sleep from her eyes, Nora hadn't understood every word. But she'd gotten the drift of their conversation—especially the part about another business trip. "When are you leaving for Taiwan?" she asked, unable to keep disappointment from surfacing in her voice.

"Tomorrow, actually." He gave her a speculative look. "I was wondering if you might like to go with me."

Her enthusiasm for the venture took a quantum leap. "Seiji...do you mean it?" she asked.

He nodded. "I wouldn't suggest it otherwise."

"Then I'd love to!" she exclaimed.

The little parentheses that framed his mouth deepened. "In that case, it's settled," he said, his smile segueing into a possessive kiss.

A half hour later, they joined their guests at the breakfast table. Happier than she could remember being, though the tenor of her relationship with Seiji was still very much in flux and she didn't have any real notion of whether he reciprocated her feelings, Nora beamed at everyone.

In his own, somewhat less effusive way, Seiji was beaming, too. "She eats cereal instead of a proper breakfast," he noted, poking fun at her with extraordinary good humor. "Can you believe it? No miso soup and rice...not even a pickle! How will we ever make healthy babies together?"

They'd been speaking a mixture of Japanese and English, and he'd chosen to comment in the latter tongue for her benefit. His words prompted a buried question to nibble at the edge of Nora's consciousness. It retreated along with her slight frown when someone laughingly shushed him in Japanese, once again forcing her to put her newly acquired language skills to the test.

Before long, they were bidding their guests farewell and getting into the limousine while Harumi placed their luggage in the trunk, locked up the house and got behind the wheel. The weather was fine and the traffic light as they started for Kyoto.

"So," said Seiji, declining even to glance at the current financial magazines and assorted paperwork he'd placed in one of the leather seatpockets the previous morning. "What shall we do to amuse ourselves during the journey?"

Nora wondered what he was suggesting. A game of cards, perhaps? She doubted they were conversant with the same ones, with the possible exception of bridge and poker. "I don't have the slightest idea," she admitted.

"In that case," he said, "let me propose something." Switching off his cellular phone so they wouldn't be disturbed, he inserted a hand under her denim miniskirt.

Matched only by her appetite for him, Nora's embarrassment knew no bounds. She might be a married woman, by now thoroughly initiated in the ways of lovemaking. But she wasn't bold enough to enjoy scandalizing a third party. "Seiji...*please!*" she whispered. "What will Harumi think?"

"Nothing, if he can't see us."

With the press of a button, he caused a panel to slide noiselessly into place, shielding the back seat from the chauffeur's gaze.

I wonder how many times he's called that particular feature of the limousine into play to ensure his privacy with a woman passenger, Nora thought. Tamao, for instance. Or Haruko. Yet he hadn't married either of them.

She vowed not to let thoughts of them intrude. "The question is," she said shakily, "whether he'll be able to see the cars behind us as well as those in front of us.''

''The limo has side mirrors.''

Giving her a protracted, openmouthed kiss, Seiji deftly maneuvered her panties down to her ankles. ''Take them off all the way, darling, and straddle my lap on your pretty knees,'' he suggested. A moment later, he'd unzipped his fly and allowed his engorged manhood to spring free. Reaching into his pocket, he slipped on protection.

''Granted it's been an amorous weekend,'' he added, his voice rough with anticipation. ''But I haven't begun to get enough.''

With a helpless little moan, Nora covered him and drew him into her depths. Amazingly quick to arousal despite the short time she and Seiji had been together, her most sensitive places were clamoring for fulfillment. I've never known such desire, such extraordinary bliss, she thought, catching an occasional, haphazard glimpse of the traffic behind them through the limo's smoked-glass rear window as they bumped and ground, invaded and tightened, creating an erotic paradise for each other.

Incredibly, they made love three times during their journey. Nora was weak-kneed, her bones like water from a surfeit of ecstasy by the time they reached the gravel turnaround in front of Seiji's Kyoto house.

Summoned by one of the servants, perhaps, Aiko came to the *genkan* or entry vestibule to greet them. The expression on her face caused a little knot of worry to form in Nora's stomach.

''I tried to call, but your cell phone didn't seem to be working,'' she greeted her son in Japanese with a sidelong glance in Nora's direction. ''Your wife's sister phoned. Her aunt's condition has worsened. They've taken her back to the hospital.''

His expression suddenly very sober, Seiji translated with one arm about Nora's shoulders.

"Oh, no!'' she cried, huge tears rolling down her cheeks. "She can't die...not now, when Braet & Company is going to make it!''

If her wail of disbelief at the irony of the situation threatened his feeling that they'd reached an understanding apart from their agreed-upon year of marriage, he didn't say so. "Which sister was it, Mother?'' he asked calmly in English. "Stephanie? Or Darien?''

Aiko replied that it had been the latter. She addressed herself to Nora. "I'm very sorry to be the bearer of such bad news,'' she said with obvious sincerity. "Your sister told me that, by the time you called her back, she'd be at the hospital. Apparently she's a doctor there. She said you could reach her in your aunt's room. Or, failing that, the emergency department.''

Nora turned to Seiji. "I'll have to go,'' she said, silently begging him to understand.

He didn't voice any objection. "You'd better call your sister at once,'' he suggested. "I'll use my cell phone to make your flight reservations.''

He isn't going with me, she realized. Maybe he won't come at all. Does this mean our separation will be permanent?

It was as if she'd put her doubts and misgivings into words. "I hope you won't mind if I don't make the trip with you at once,'' he said, tightening his grip. "We don't know for a fact, yet, how serious your aunt's situation is. It could drag on for weeks. Meanwhile, my business in Taipei is fairly important. If necessary, I can be on a plane to the States by Wednesday evening.''

It would have to do.

''Thanks...I appreciate your willingness to join me when you can,'' Nora said in a small voice, the certainty that her aunt wasn't going to make it chilling her to the bone. ''I'll keep you informed of what's happening.'' She paused. ''I guess I'd better phone Darien.''

Her heart sank even further when Darien confirmed her worst fears. Maggie was dying. Her doctors weren't holding out any hope.

''Her tumors have progressed to the point that her trachea isn't midline any longer,'' Darien said with a slight tremor in her voice. ''Both lungs are fully involved. She's having a great deal of difficulty breathing, despite a fairly heavy dose of oxygen. Plus there's some indication the cancer has spread to her neck and shoulders. Her pulmonary specialist and her oncologist agree. It's likely to be just a matter of days...''

As she listened, Nora was weeping. ''I'm coming home, of course,'' she said when Darien fell silent. ''Seiji's on his cell phone now, making my airline reservations. I want to be with her to the last.''

They arranged that Nora would call back with her flight number and time of arrival as soon as they were available. But, ''I don't want you to leave her side in order to meet me at the airport,'' Nora insisted. ''If Steph can't come after me, I'll take a taxi. Making things easier for Maggie is the only thing I care about.''

Returning to the house, Seiji announced that he'd managed to get her a flight that evening from Narita Airport in Tokyo. ''We'll have to step on it,'' he warned, unconsciously resorting to an American slang expression he'd picked up at Harvard. "I've alerted Harumi. You've got approximately five minutes to throw some clothes into a suitcase."

He accompanied her to the airport in his limo. Holding tightly to his hand, Nora rested her head on his shoulder as they burned up the miles that separated Kyoto and Tokyo. When I arrived in Japan, Seiji was my opponent in a chess game of vengeance, reward and lust, she thought. Now my feelings for him have become so complex, so utterly deep. I'd give anything if he could come with me, be at my side when I have to face the changes in Maggie, prepare myself for her death.

Thanks to the clarity of perspective forced on her by Darien's devastating news, she had realized beyond the shadow of a doubt that she was in love with him. If it's what he wants and he can manage to remain faithful, I want to stay married to him, she thought. Have the babies he talked about. I'd want them to grow up in the States of course, at least part of the time. We'd need homes in several places.

With no words of commitment between them, or any discussion of what the future might bring, the days ahead were like blank pages on a calendar. She couldn't predict what they might hold.

Though she couldn't know it, her dark-haired husband was wrestling with similar thoughts and insecurities of his own. I wonder if she'll want me at her side after she's been back in America for a few days, he thought. The *Braets* certainly won't. To them, I'm the ultimate outsider, the despised end product of Jerrold Braet's extramarital fling with a twenty-two-year-old

Japanese girl that broke his wife's heart. They'll be only too pleased if Nora repudiates our marriage...files for a quick divorce, now that she has no pressing reason to continue it.

Ironically, with that possibility at hand, he'd begun to realize how much it would devastate him to lose her. Even the idea of gaining his longed-for retaliation at her expense had become anathema to him. I'm beginning to want a genuine marriage with her, one that has a decent chance of lasting, he thought. Maybe even the children I teased her about. Though he refused to put a name to the fever that was circulating in his bloodstream, he'd begun to suspect it was love—a strong and selfish emotion that made him reluctant to let her go as he accompanied her into the terminal.

Harumi had burned up the pavement between Kyoto and Tokyo and as a result, they were a few minutes early. After checking in at the airline counter and again at the gate, they sat together in the waiting area, with his arm around her shoulders. Neither of them seemed to know what to say to the other.

Though most of Nora's thoughts were with Maggie, compounded of sorrow and an overwhelming urge to hold her aunt's wasted body in her arms, she was keenly focused on Seiji, too. Part of her couldn't bear to leave him. Yet, aside from his desire for intercourse with her and the unexpected kindness he'd recently displayed, she had no idea what he felt.

Since running into each other at Mishikikaji Market, she and Rosemary Pennington had met several times for lunch. Now, as she glanced surreptitiously at Seiji's profile, something her friend had said in passing leapt to the forefront of her consciousness.

"In Japan," Rosemary had commented, "children…especially males…are taught to maintain their composure no matter what. They learn to hide their tender feelings under multiple layers of self-control. As a result, sometimes they themselves don't have a clue to them.''

Though Seiji was only one-quarter Japanese, he'd been brought up in Japan until it was time for him to go away to school. In all likelihood, he'd learned how to deal with emotions from Aiko. From the sparse accounts of his childhood he'd shared, his Danish-Norwegian father had been largely absent from their lives.

Even if he came to love me, he might not know it, Nora realized. We still might find ourselves continents apart, both physically and in our feelings.

Abruptly her flight was called. Since Seiji had purchased a luxury-class seat for her, Nora's row was among those called first. He walked with her as far as the podium, where she'd be required to show her boarding pass.

She was second in line when he pulled her into his arms. ''Have a safe flight,'' he said gruffly, intermittently speaking and kissing her mouth. ''I'll call you late tomorrow evening…at your sister Darien's place. Or your aunt's condo, if there's no answer there. I've got both numbers in my wallet. If you want me at your side, I can start for Seattle on Wednesday evening. You have only to let me know.''

Seconds later, he was releasing her. She was turning and walking like an automaton down the jetway. Halfway to the plane, she paused and glanced over her shoulder. He was still standing where she'd left him, gazing after her with a difficult-to-read expression on his face.

* * *

It was overcast with a hint of rain in the air when they landed in Seattle the following morning. Stephanie wasn't waiting at the gate. Grateful she hadn't brought much luggage, Nora grabbed a cab and headed for the hospital.

Assigned to a private room on the pulmonary floor, Maggie was a ghost of her former self. She looked at least twenty years older. Her complexion was ashen. The cords in her neck stood out from her struggle for breath. An oxygen cannula made of transparent green plastic tubing had been fitted into her nostrils.

Always slender, she'd lost an enormous amount of weight. Her formerly expressive hands were limp, blue-veined and skeletal. Only her eyes, which for once weren't framed by her usual tortoise-rimmed glasses, held a glimpse of her fighting spirit.

"Nora...darling!" she exclaimed in a hoarse whisper. "It's so good to see you. I only wish I didn't have to be so sick to lure you back from Japan."

"Oh, Maggie...I wish you didn't, either! I should have come back sooner..."

A moment later, they were embracing, lightly but desperately because of Maggie's fragile state.

"Sit down and talk, sweet girl. I want to hear everything," Maggie said at last, releasing her and lightly patting the coverlet. "About your modeling in Japan and your romance with Mr. Amundsen. Don't leave out a single detail."

In the ways that counted, she was just the same— loving, enamored of gossip, profoundly interested in everything that was happening in her nieces' lives. I wonder if she knows the truth about her condition,

Nora thought. Surely Darien's seen to it that they've told her, so she can prepare herself.

Pulling up a chair so she wouldn't take up any of her aunt's comfort space, Nora made up modeling assignments that had never taken place. She portrayed Seiji as a powerful, vibrant man, admitting that she'd fallen deeply in love with him.

"Don't tell Dad," she said. "But we got married." Suspecting Maggie hadn't noticed them yet, she held up her engagement and wedding rings for her aunt's inspection.

Maggie gazed at the rings admiringly. "Darling!" she exclaimed. "I'm so happy for you!"

More hugs followed, diminished only by Maggie's frailty. At last Nora's aunt sank back against the pillows. "I can't wait to meet him," she said in her wispy voice. "Will he be visiting soon?"

Though she yearned to have Seiji at her side, absorb the deep comfort of his hard, tall body into the place where it hurt the most, Nora hadn't been able to convince herself his coming would be a good idea. Forced to see and deal with him, her father might blow a gasket. So might a number of her other Braet relatives. Meanwhile, open war among her family members was the last thing Maggie needed to deal with at the moment.

"He offered to fly over Wednesday evening," she answered. "I have only to say the word. I'm afraid his presence here might cause some problems."

Despite the gravity of her condition, which might have sapped the will of a lesser person, Maggie was adamant. She wanted to meet Seiji as soon as possible. "If we wait, I might not be around to help welcome him to the family," she said. "Of course we're already relatives in more ways than one...if he's crazy enough to want us.''

Tears pricked Nora's eyelids. Maggie can't die, she thought. I won't let her! Something willful and childish in her wanted to keep up the pretense that everything would be okay.

''Maybe he could come at Christmas,'' she persisted. ''That's less than two months away.''

Maggie cupped her chin with emaciated fingers. ''Sorry. But I'm dying, sweet child,'' she said, holding Nora's gaze so firmly with her own that she couldn't seek refuge in the weepy-looking clouds outside the room's small window or the profusion of medical equipment that surrounded her aunt's bed like a phalanx of robots.

''We have to face it, darling,'' Maggie added firmly, albeit with tears in her eyes. ''I'm not in any position to make long-range commitments.''

Nora was deeply depressed and exhausted—overwhelmed by a bone-deep sense of helplessness as she crashed on one of the sofas in Maggie's Lake Union condo that evening and stared out the living room's sliding glass doors. The panorama of sailboats and choppy water they revealed didn't offer any answers or life-preserving formulas.

Maggie won't return to gaze at this view again, she realized. She'll spend her last days in the sterile environment of a hospital room, saying goodbye to everyone and everything she loves. Heartsick to the core, Nora longed to feel Seiji's strong arms around her.

Suddenly the phone rang. *Was it the hospital calling?* She'd left Maggie's home number with the night staff, impressing them with the need to phone her at once if there was any change in her aunt's condition.

"Hello?" she blurted, snatching up the receiver.

"Hi...it's Seiji," he said.

Though his pleasantly deep voice was like honey in her ear, it couldn't assuage the grief she felt.

"I'm still in Taipei," he added. "How's your aunt doing?"

Nora didn't answer immediately. Then, "She's dying," she confessed. "We could lose her at any moment."

"What can I do?" he asked. "If it's anything money can fix..."

"It isn't. But thank you for asking."

New to a genuinely caring relationship, Seiji felt like a fool for having suggested anything of the sort. "Look," he said, searching for a way to comfort her with so much distance between them, "I'm confirmed on a flight to Seattle, departing tomorrow evening. When I get there, I'll take a taxi straight to the hospital."

He'd keep his promise. A shiver of relief passed through her. "Call me here first, or in Maggie's hospital room," she instructed, better able to handle her negative emotions, thanks to the prospect of his support. "I have the use of Maggie's car. If I can leave her bedside, I'll pick you up at the airport."

He was airborne somewhere over the Pacific when Maggie died at 3:47 a.m. Seattle time.

Nora was alone with her during her final moments. Both Stephanie and Darien had gone to the latter's apartment several hours earlier to catch some sleep. Simultaneously Maggie's doctor had been summoned

to treat another critical, but not moribund patient. Since
there was nothing more they could do, Nora had asked
the nurse to leave the room as well.

Unsure how she'd handle the process of her aunt's
dying, Nora got through it dry-eyed by speaking softly
to Maggie about the outings they'd enjoyed when she
was small and Maggie had functioned as her surrogate
mom amid an ever-changing panoply of stepmothers.
Over and over, she told her aunt how much she loved
her, and promised that they'd see each other again
someday. It was only afterward, when Maggie's struggle had ceased and one of the nurses returned to ease
her from the room, that she began to weep in earnest.

Parking in one of the airport lots approximately six
hours later, Nora walked to the international terminal.
Her dark-haired husband, who always traveled first-
class, was one of the first passengers to deplane.

The look on her face told him what had happened.
"Come here," he said roughly, setting his garment bag
aside and pulling her into his embrace.

The days leading up to Maggie's funeral were difficult for her nieces, especially Nora, who'd been the
closest to her. Seiji's presence seemed to help. The
quiet strength and take-charge ability that had both re-
pelled and attracted her from the beginning now
seemed unmitigated assets.

For the time being, they remained at Maggie's condo
to maintain some privacy. It was quickly apparent,
however, that they needn't have worried about out-
raged parents, uncles and cousins knocking at their
door. Their only visitors were Stephanie and Darien,
who treated their new brother-in-law with equanimity,

together with five or six floral delivery people and a representative from the funeral home they'd chosen.

While Nora and her sisters busied themselves with the necessary arrangements, Seiji remained quietly by, conducting his usual business transactions by phone whenever the condo's single line was free and performing little services for them.

So quickly Nora could scarcely believe it possible, the morning of Maggie's funeral arrived. Having held her in a nonsexual way the night before as she'd cried herself to sleep, Seiji laced his fingers through hers and provided her with a shoulder to lean on at the church, especially during a eulogy by Maggie's favorite clergyman. He was there for her at the cemetery as well, somber in his dark suit and raincoat as he rested a hand protectively on her shoulder.

Well aware of the dislike and open hostility Nora's father, Stephen Braet, and some of her other relatives were directing toward him, Seiji was careful not to register any emotion. How things have changed! he thought with a mental shake of his head. Before I met Nora, I'd never have tolerated this kind of treatment from anyone. *Especially* not the Braets. Now I'm willing to put my pride in my pocket.

He and Nora had come a long way from their initial bargain and the realization gladdened him despite the sympathy he felt. Yet he knew it was still possible that, with Maggie out of the picture, Nora might retreat from him. She certainly didn't need his Braet & Company stock any longer. When she recovered from her loss, she might hand him his walking papers.

The graveside service was typical of Seattle in that it started to rain and a sea of black umbrellas opened. Reverently, gently, surrounded by the love and respect of her family, friends and employees, Maggie was laid to rest. It was time to leave her flower-heaped grave for an informal get-together at Nora's father's clifftop home, which overlooked Puget Sound in Seattle's wealthy Magnolia section.

Despite his wife's whispered pleas to stop, Stephen Braet had been swigging bourbon from a silver flask throughout the burial. Now, to Nora's revulsion and dismay, as everyone started back toward their cars, he announced in a booming, unquestionably slurred voice, "I don't want that rich, smart-ass Jap of Nora's in our house!"

Nora could feel Seiji stiffen. He was clearly furious. In response, she tightened her hand on his arm. "I'm not going to call him on it now out of respect for my aunt's memory," she whispered. "But I'll never speak to him again unless he apologizes to your satisfaction. Please...take me back to Aunt Maggie's apartment. I want it to be just the two of us."

Amazingly she was choosing him over her father. Does that mean she actually cares for me? he wondered. That she wants me to continue as her husband? Banking the fire of his displeasure, he did what she asked.

The phone was ringing when they walked in. Taking it off the hook, Nora wrapped it in a dish towel and stuffed it into a drawer. Seiji helped her off with her raincoat. While she went into the bedroom to change, he removed his own raincoat and jacket as well, and hung all three garments in the hall closet. Building a fire in Maggie's fifties' modern fireplace, he fixed a Scotch for each of them.

Nora returned to the living room after some minutes

wearing one of her aunt's favorite kimono-style robes. Its former owner's scent still clung to it.

"She loved everything Japanese, especially the art and decorative fabrics," she said, smoothing the flowered silk with her fingertips as she sat beside Seiji on the couch. "Unfortunately she never traveled to your country. I think she might have come to visit us...that is, if she'd gotten better...."

Choking off the most forlorn words he'd ever heard from her mouth, she gazed at him with tear-filled eyes. Not knowing any other way to comfort her, he drew her close.

It was what she wanted. "I'm going to miss her so," she quavered. Seconds later, she was sobbing her heart out as she buried her face against his shirt.

According to Maggie's lawyer, who'd attended the funeral, Nora had been chosen as her aunt's executor. "With you based in Japan these days," he told her on the phone the following morning, "I can handle most of the details. However, I'm going to need you to sign some papers. And go through her things. Though she made a will, to my knowledge she didn't leave a 'separate writing' disposing of her personal possessions."

Maggie Braet had been a pack rat when it came to Japanese and contemporary paintings, expensive jewelry and books. Some of the overflow had been placed in rented storage bins. It's going to take days, if not *weeks*, Nora thought despairingly. Meanwhile, Seiji had an important meeting coming up in Tokyo.

He postponed it once for my sake already, in order to join me here, she reminded herself. I don't want him to feel he has to hang around in Seattle just to prop me up.

Baring her thoughts to him, she insisted he fly back to Japan on Monday. "I'll join you there just as soon as I can," she promised, her mouth gravitating to his.

About to protest, Seiji stopped to think that, in his absence, she'd be able to spend more time with her family, especially her sisters. Reluctantly he agreed with the suggestion. Their kisses were fierce, almost desperate two days later when they parted at Sea-Tac Airport.

Leaning back in his seat as he waited for his plane to take off, he wondered if he was making a mistake by leaving. Because of the arranged nature of their marriage and the awkwardness it entailed, they still hadn't spoken any love words to each other. Though by this time he knew his own feelings well enough, he was by no means certain of hers. With her reason for marrying him gone, he could only hope she'd return to him.

Stuck in Seattle for the next three weeks handling the estate, Nora was almost ready to fly back to Japan when she received a small package in the mail. It was postmarked Kyoto. Seiji's sent me a present! she thought, feeling a burst of enthusiasm and pleasure for the first time since her aunt's death.

Instead of a gift from her husband, the package contained an amateur videotape of him and Haruko Nakanishi affectionately strolling the grounds of Kinkakuji Temple. "I thought you should know. They're seeing each other again," the accompanying note declared. Unsigned, it had been neatly written in a rounded, girlish hand on a sheet of rice-paper stationery.

Nora guessed at once that the note and videotape had been sent by the mistress before Haruko. To think that all the while, he'd been phoning daily and acting as if he cared for her!

Inconsolable over Maggie's death and aghast at the idea that Seiji had been unfaithful, Nora didn't stop to reason things out. Or express some healthy skepticism. It was the same demeaning injury her father had done to his assorted wives, the way Jerrold had callously broken her great-grandmother's heart. She didn't plan to abide it—not for a single second.

Within minutes, she was driving downtown and handing the videotape and note to her aunt's attorney.

"I want you to write my husband and demand that he give me a divorce on the grounds of infidelity," she said with a furious glint in eyes that were red and swollen from excessive weeping. "Include a duplicate of this videotape and note as evidence of my claim. This is a notarized copy of our marriage contract for your reference. You can tell him to stuff his Braet & Company stock wherever he deems appropriate!"

Two days later, she flew to New York, where she sublet an apartment on a month-to-month basis, requested an unlisted phone number and hired a moving company to retrieve her furniture and possessions from storage. Far from helping to heal her wounds, the defensive legal action she'd taken against Seiji only had made her feel worse. It was as if the world had crashed into little pieces at her feet.

No amount of antacid tablets seemed able to settle her upset stomach. In despair, she made an appointment to see her doctor. It was only in his examining room, when he inquired about the timing of her last period, that she realized she must be pregnant.

Chapter Twelve

For months later, as Nora was about to enter the sixth month of her pregnancy, she felt great physically. Emotionally, though she was overjoyed at the thought of becoming a mother, her heart was still a basket case over what she believed had been the treachery of the man she loved.

To her surprise, he'd done nothing to counter her attorney's letter. There'd been no phone calls. No coldly worded missives insisting she carry out their contract or face a lawsuit. No rages or denials. No sweet talk in her living room. For her part, she'd taken no further action, believing a child's parents ought to be married to each other when he or she came into the world.

Part of her refused to believe what she considered his former mistress's charges and continued to hope their marriage could be saved. Still, she planned to keep her pregnancy and their baby's impending birth a secret from him—to the degree possible now that she was working again. The thought of fighting a custody battle with him chilled her to the bone. All of Seiji's training had programmed him to win any conflict in which he might find himself. As much as he meant to her, and he meant a lot, the helpless little being whose movements fluttered beneath her heart took precedence.

If he finds out we made a child when we consummated our marriage, she thought, he'll initiate a tug-of-war like the one Steph, Darien and I were forced to endure between Mom and Dad until Mom was killed in that five-car accident.

In Kyoto or wherever he happened to be, Seiji suffered from a bone-deep melancholy. Without Nora, his life seemed etched in shades of gray. Nothing, not even the most adept and remunerative business triumph, seemed to hold any meaning for him.

His original fury on receiving her attorney's letter, the video tape that had accompanied it, and what appeared to be a childishly written note on rice paper, had faded. He hadn't responded to her request for a divorce and there'd been no follow-up. The videotape's origin continued to puzzle him. Who had taken the trouble to record his stroll with Haruko through Kinkakuji Temple grounds a year and a half earlier? The likely culprit was Tamao, who'd been outspoken about her jealousy of his brief romance with her successor. Of course Tamao had denied it when he'd demanded the truth.

Surely Nora realized the 'evidence' she'd received was false, perpetrated by someone with something to gain from it. Maybe her father had sent a detective to Japan to interview his acquaintances and business associates—one who'd turned up a tape someone else had planned to use against him.

Whatever the case, he believed that, with Maggie Braet gone, Nora had asked to be released from their marriage because she saw no reason to continue it. Though he was puzzled that she hadn't taken any further action, he had too much pride to contact her. Ironic, isn't it? he thought one night as he soaked in his wooden tub preparatory to turning in. *I inveigled her into marriage as a way of punishing and humiliating her family, and ended up loving her. For the first time in my life, since parting from her at Sea-Tac, I've remained celibate.*

With a sigh that came from the depths of his soul, he picked up his TV remote control and flipped on CNN. Following an ad, he found himself watching an Elsa Klench fashion segment. It appeared to be about the new look in maternity clothes.

About to change channels, he was suddenly immobilized by the sight of Nora striding fluidly down the runway with the unmistakably distended belly of an expectant mother. It could be padding, he thought as he stared at her. But instinctively he knew better. She was having his baby!

A half second later, the camera cut to a dark-haired model, also padded or expecting. *It happened the first time we made love, the* only *time I forgot to use protection,* Seiji exulted. *And now we're inextricably linked.*

Did she parade on television that way because she wanted me to see her and beg her to come back to me? he wondered. *Or just assume that I didn't watch fashion shows?*

The answer was immaterial. Whatever her reasons

for wanting a divorce, he'd counter them. Convince her they were smoke and mirrors. He loved her, dammit! And wanted them to raise their child together.

With his gaze still focused on the screen in case Nora should reappear, he reached for the phone to order himself a plane ticket. I've got to get her back, he thought as he waited for an agent to come on the line. There was a time when I thought I had a decent chance with her.

When he arrived in New York a few days later, Seiji called on Nora's agent. Despite considerable persuasion on his part, the woman refused his demands for his wife's home address. However, she unbent sufficiently to tell him Nora was doing a fashion shoot at that very moment. Additional coaxing elicited the address. Promising the agent a dozen roses or a mink coat, whichever she preferred, he hailed his chauffeur.

He was lucky enough to find the receptionist's post deserted when he arrived at the photographer's third-floor suite. A glance at his watch told him it was approaching the lunch hour. After a quick look around that took in the water cooler and a pay phone attached to one wall, he walked quietly into the connecting studio.

The area just inside the door was dark, unlit in stark contrast to the powerful brilliance of the klieg lights that surrounded Nora like a halo. Her belly even bigger than it had appeared on CNN as she modeled a clingy, oversize top and matching leggings in sharp citrus colors, she turned this way and that, smiling, tossing her head and running her fingers through her hair with supple grace in response to the photographer's instructions.

Remaining in shadow, Seiji felt his heart turn over

in his chest. She was so unbelievably damn radiant. Even more than I remember her being, he acknowledged, now that she's carrying our baby. I need her to live, not just exist. Somehow I've got to convince her I didn't trash our marriage vows...that I can do whatever it takes to make her happy.

With the thought a strategy occurred to him. Retreating to the pay phone in the reception area, he sent her a telegram announcing he was in the studio. The session lasted another twenty minutes, including a pause so Nora could sip some of the bottled water she'd tucked into her backpack.

His telegram was delivered just as she and the photographer were about to pause for lunch. Seiji watched from the shadows as she opened it. He all but held his breath as she read the brief message it contained and glanced up to visually search the darker reaches of the studio beyond the klieg lights.

Blinded by their brilliance, she was stunned at the news that Seiji was there, in New York, in that very room. Had he come to talk about her request for a divorce? Or something she didn't dare dream about?

Whatever the case, he'd discovered by now that she was pregnant. Seconds later, she walked off the set as if drawn by a tractor beam despite the photographer's protest of "Just a couple more shots in that outfit. Okay, Nora? Then we'll break..."

She ignored him totally. By then, she'd spotted Seiji. Approaching to within a few feet of him, she hesitated, as if afraid to take another step.

In the end, the right words came to him.

"Just look at you," he murmured with a little shake of his head. "You're out to *here*." All the love he felt for her resonated in his voice as he held out his arms.

With a little shudder at how right it felt, she came into them. They'd save the postmortems for later. Everything his cast-off mistress said was a lie, she realized as his mouth covered hers. He was never unfaithful. What a fool I was, playing into Tamao's hands!

His kiss was like the earth, huge and sheltering. She wanted to drown in its immensity, seek its shelter. For her, he was the sun, the moon, the north star's steady beacon.

At last, holding her back from him so he could gaze into her eyes, he told her how much he loved her. "Since the moment you came into my life, there's never been another woman for me," he assured her. "I love you...and our baby...so much."

Tears of happiness rolled down her cheeks. "I love you, too," she whispered.

They were kissing again, deeply and eagerly, when the photographer interrupted them to suggest he and Nora start their lunch break immediately. "If you can," he told her, "try to be back by 2:00 p.m. If you can't, I'll expect you when I see you."

A minute or two later, she and Seiji were hugging on the sidewalk. "What made you come after me, considering the way I treated you?" she asked.

His love for her was overflowing. "I saw you on television," he said. "Modeling maternity outfits. It was like a catalyst."

Was it just the baby that had motivated him? Determined to learn from her mistakes, Nora chased the unworthy thought from her head. Just then, the little person in question moved. On impulse, she placed Seiji's hand on her abdomen.

His gray eyes glittering suspiciously, he shook his

head. "That was a pretty strong kick," he said. "He or she is going to be a terror."

Nora smiled. "Just like his father."

He considered her comment for a moment. "So…it's going to be a boy," he said at last.

She confirmed his speculation.

"I'm Westernized enough that a girl would please me just as much," he said. "If you like, we can have one next time."

As he held her close, he couldn't help recalling the pleasures of their first lovemaking. I took a virgin and made her into a mother that night, he thought. "It looks as if I won't be able to make love to you for some time," he said regretfully.

At that, Nora broke into the wide smile that had done so much to boost her career. "Ah, but I can make love to *you*," she countered. "We can go to my place. Or rent a hotel room for an hour. I want to kiss you all over."

* * * * *

Take 2 bestselling love stories FREE

Plus get a FREE surprise gift!

Special Limited-Time Offer

Mail to Silhouette Reader Service™

3010 Walden Avenue
P.O. Box 1867
Buffalo, N.Y. 14240-1867

YES! Please send me 2 free Silhouette Romance™ novels and my free surprise gift. Then send me 6 brand-new novels every month, which I will receive months before they appear in bookstores. Bill me at the low price of $2.90 each plus 25¢ delivery and applicable sales tax, if any.* That's the complete price, and a saving of over 10% off the cover prices—quite a bargain! I understand that accepting the books and gift places me under no obligation ever to buy any books. I can always return a shipment and cancel at any time. Even if I never buy another book from Silhouette, the 2 free books and the surprise gift are mine to keep forever.

215 SEN CH7S

Name	(PLEASE PRINT)	
Address	Apt. No.	
City	State	Zip

This offer is limited to one order per household and not valid to present Silhouette Romance™ subscribers. *Terms and prices are subject to change without notice. Sales tax applicable in N.Y.

USROM-98   ©1990 Harlequin Enterprises Limited

Maternity Leave

Coming September 1998

Three delightful stories about the blessings
and surprises of "Labor" Day.

TABLOID BABY by Candace Camp

She was whisked to the hospital in the nick of time....

THE NINE-MONTH KNIGHT
by Cait London

A down-on-her-luck secretary is experiencing
odd little midnight cravings....

THE PATERNITY TEST by Sherryl Woods

The stick turned blue before her
biological clock struck twelve....

*These three special women are very pregnant...and very
single, although they won't be either for too much longer,
because baby—and Daddy—are on their way!*

Available at your favorite retail outlet.

FIVE STARS
MEAN SUCCESS

If you see the "5 Star Club" flash on a book,
it means we're introducing you to one of our
most STELLAR authors!

Every one of our Harlequin and Silhouette
authors who has sold over 5 MILLION BOOKS
has been selected for our "5 Star Club."

We've created the club so you won't miss
any of our bestsellers. So, each month
we'll be highlighting every original book within
Harlequin and Silhouette written by our
bestselling authors.

NOW THERE'S NO WAY ON EARTH OUR STARS WON'T BE SEEN!

OVER
5 MILLION
BOOKS SOLD
SPECIAL OFFER INSIDE

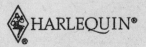

HARLEQUIN®   Silhouette®

P5STAR

The World's Most Eligible Bachelors are about to be named! And Silhouette Books brings them to you in an all-new, original series....

World's Most Eligible Bachelors

Twelve of the sexiest, most sought-after men share every intimate detail of their lives in twelve never-before-published novels by the genre's top authors.

Don't miss these unforgettable stories by:

Dixie Browning

Marie Ferrarella

Jackie Merritt

Tracy Sinclair

BJ James

RACHEL LEE

Suzanne Carey

Gina Wilkins

VICTORIA PADE

MAGGIE SHAYNE

Anne McAllister

Susan Mallery

Look for one new book each month in the **World's Most Eligible Bachelors** series beginning September 1998 from Silhouette Books.

Silhouette®

Available at your favorite retail outlet.

Our **5 Star Club** authors are successful authors who have sold *over 5 million books*. In honor of their success, we're offering you a __FREE__ gift and a chance to look like a million bucks!

You can choose:

the necklace...

the bracelet...

or the earrings...

Or indulge, and receive all three!

To receive one item, send in 1 (one)* proof of purchase, plus $1.65 U.S./$2.25 CAN. for postage and handling, to:

In the U.S.	**In Canada**
Harlequin 5 Star Club	Harlequin 5 Star Club
3010 Walden Ave.	P.O. Box 636
P.O. Box 9047	Fort Erie, Ontario
Buffalo, NY	L2A 5X3
14269-9047	

* To receive more than one piece of jewelry, send in another proof of purchase and an additional 25¢ for each extra item.

---

5 STAR CLUB—
PROOF OF PURCHASE

Inventory:	Item:	
721-1	Necklace	☐
722-9	Bracelet	☐
723-7	Earrings	☐

Name: _____

Address: _____

City: _____

State/Prov.: _____ Zip/Postal Code: _____

Account number:_____ (if applicable)

093 KGI CFKZ   *Silhouette*®

093 KGI CFKZ